Kraken

Prelusion

Cai arrived in Zurich again and checked into the *Baur au Lac Hotel*. He sat down in the hotel lobby and began to reflect on Switzerland.

Undoubtedly, Zurich today is a beautiful and developed city, but this was not always the case. Archibald made it his third favorite city on this Earth. Here you rarely can see happy faces; everyone is gloomy and perplexed by the problems of everyday life and making money. Money is the most important issue in Switzerland. If in a Russian godforsaken backward village grubby *mouzhiks*-peasants gulp by full glasses rough potato *moonshine*, they toast to love and health, so that God will give and help them. There is no money at all, but people laugh more than in well-fed Switzerland. Soon everywhere it will be like in Switzerland.

Cai looked at the coffee table and saw the German magazine *Der Spiegel*. It used to be a very interesting magazine, and Cai liked to read this particular periodical, he considered it one of the best. On the front page, he saw a photo of Kadarkovsky, and was curious, because he knew him personally. Kadarkovsky was common as dirt swindler; he grew rich during the breakup of the Soviet Union by deceit and murder and wanted to come to power by any means. In 1999, this rich Russian Jew arrived in Geneva and gave an interview to the magazine *Der Spiegel*. If you carefully read and reflect on Kadarkovsky's answers, you will understand that he is a scoundrel. Surprisingly, in comparison, he had presented gifts for all politicians, for his wife he purchased a necklace for half a million dollars, but he fisted money for an orphanage. He grudged orphans the money because, according to his theory, the miserable existence of poor orphans was their *karma*, so it was improper to intervene in this situation.

Cai thought aloud, "Yeah, a nice theory, you should not interfere. Well, brat, I'll show you the damn **karma**."

Cai let saliva drip from his lip onto the photo in the magazine, and began to rub the spit with his finger upon the self-contented face of the billionaire, until he rubbed a hole and wiped his head off.

'Let us now look at your **karma**, I will not even ask Archibald, no one will even know about the existence of such a scoundrel, and no one, stinky turd, will defend you. I would grind you down into dust myself and nobody would intercede for you, "so as not to spoil your **karma**"!'

Cai's eyes turned dark and anger burst inside him. He tried to calm down. He picked up another magazine that came to his hand and began flipping through the pages. He saw an article in the original Old Russian language, which amused him. This was a telling or a Russian fishermen and seafarers' myth about the sea monster.

"The initial news that ordinary seafarers reported about this strange sea animal in the northern ocean living, was at first thought to be a fictional fable, but then, when trustworthy people found it fair and agreed with the seafarers' observations, their surprise about it increased greatly. Danish Bishop Pontoppidan describes this beast. 'Between the great number of animals in the depths of the sea living, who are either completely from our eyes concealed, or but only rarely to us visible, there is a surprising beast called **the Kraken**, the magnitude of whom all the animate beasts known to us, is by far surpassing. Our fishermen say that often, especially in the hot summer time, being several miles from the coast, in places where the estimated depth of the sea should be 80, or 100 fathoms, they sometimes found the depth actually only thirty or twenty fathoms, or even less, measured. Both from this and from the great multitude of fishes that they then come across, they conclude that the Kraken in that place on the bottom of the sea without movement should be lying. In such a case, they observe diligently, whether the depth in an equal state remains, or whether it diminishes, that judging by their fishing networks, it is very noticeable to them. They recognize the derogation of depth as a sign that the Kraken rises higher, and then they try in every possible way very quickly from such a dangerous thing at the utmost speed escape, and from this place itself move away. Moreover, indeed, after a few minutes, they see a part of this monster, which appears above the sea surface, but no one has it ever in the whole seen. The back, or the uppermost part of this beast, in a circle for one and a half time the Anglish mile extends. At first, it some small island surrounded by things like sea plants resembles; then it seems as if some exalted places like sea shoals appear, on which great many small and medium-sized fish jump, and from those beast's flanks they into the sea fall. Finally, various shining needles, or horns, rise higher, sometimes thick and high, to the masts of mediocre ships, likened. This beast in this position, having lain for some time on the surface of the sea, little by little descends into the depths of it. And in this case it causes the sailors no less danger, like when it rises; for the movement of this animated mountain brings the sea waters into a strong oscillation, and produces colossal waves, gravitating all ships them approaching, so everything into the abyss sinks.

The luminous, sublime parts of this beast are probably his members, or so to speak, hands, by means of which he moves and feeds himself. It is said that he gives off a strong smell from himself, on which fishes from far away to him flock; he allegedly a whole month without stopping eats, while another one what he eaten stools; At this time, the water around him becomes muddy and thick, in which fishes in great numbers swimming, serve him as new food again.

'In the year of 1680, a young Kraken into the stony sea strait swam, in Norwegian Kirchshpile Alstaguke located. He got his horns, or rather more probably, his trunk, by the trees growing on the seashore caught, and at the same time, he so deep into the crevices between the great sea stones went, that he could not from those himself let free. And thus, he in the same place died. His corpse occupied most of this narrow passage, and for a long time did not rot, but starting, it caused such an intolerable stench that no one could sail past it.'

"With that news of Bishop Pontoppidan, the other is according, announced about this beast recently in the Anglish Survey, (St. Iames Chronicle) in which the following about him is said.

"Someone Robert Iameson in 1774 catching herring saw together with the sailors of his ship the amazing sea beast, which, according to its description, was similar to that by Bishop Pontoppidan described, Kraken. All the people on that ship thought that the phenomenon they perceived was nothing other than a newly born island, which was about half of the Anglish mile, and up to thirty feet above the surface of the water, the width they could not estimate. This alleged by them island, to their great surprise, little by little, rose, and then oppositely to the bottom descended; and finally, among the sea waters extremely agitated, completely from their sight disappeared. Soon afterwards, on the same spot, they found so many herrings and other fishes that they almost the full ship with them loaded. The tale from this people in court under an oath was taken, and into court records introduced."

Shutting the periodical, Cai smiled and thought, 'I'll take **Kraken** for my last name. People will dignify me as Mr. Kraken. They will immediately see who they are dealing with.'

For Cai, his long ago given name, the time itself and the life in general, have lost their meaning; he always remained strong and young. He always succeeded having a very influential support, about which no one knew. Moreover, hardly anyone would have believed. In the world of materialism, people believe in what they see with their own eyes only. Cai was fabulously rich, but money never interested him. He could afford any luxury and settle in any prestigious hotel. He traveled all over the world and stopped in Zurich; Cai put before himself the task of creating a new powerful and influential organization. Now he had an appointment at the *Baur au Lac Hotel*. He chose this hotel not at random.

Sometime back in 1814 a young lad from Austria, a baker by profession, arrived in Zurich. His parents gave him this profession so that he could survive and always feed himself. He arrived in Zurich with two copper *kreutzers* in his pocket and with a knapsack in the hope of earning some money for life. His name was Johannes Bauer, and after some time, he would build this hotel *Baur au lac* by the lake. If Johannes could foresee the cost of this hotel and his future wealth, he probably would have chosen to remain poor.

Cai for some time had been hanging out in Zurich preparing new scenarios for revolutions. The people demanded stability, and after Napoleon Bonaparte was discharged, everyone had to think about their independent state. In Vienna, a meeting was scheduled with the representatives of the revolutionary cells, they needed money, and Cai decided to support them. His eternal companion and friend Archibald was always glad to push human beings to ram together with their foreheads so as to shed blood in large quantities; then people would sin more and move away from God. Archibald loved to have fun and did not spare money for it.

Johannes

Poor Johannes, hungry, shabby and dirty, hung around the streets looking for a job. He could not find any work, and had to spend the night, hiding in a back street, hoping for a miracle. Johannes was a faithful believer because his parents gave him a Catholic education; he was baptized in a church and had a silver cross hanging on a silver chain around his neck.

Our friend Cai was in a hurry and was heading for his carriage at a brisk pace, not paying attention to a thin and dirty ragged young man whom he pushed in full force. The guy fell on the pavement, hurting his head. Cai stopped at once and helped the derelict get on his feet. Johannes felt unwell, he recognized that he could be beaten or handed over to the *jägers*, and then he would have a tough time.

However, Johannes was very lucky. He met Cai and all his life has changed forever. Cai glanced at young Johannes and asked, "Do you want to eat?"

Hot buns were sold nearby, and Cai bought some fresh bread for the guy. He saw a solemn servant-to-be standing before him.

Cai asked, "Do you need a job, young fellow?"

Johannes nodded his head repeatedly, he was afraid to scare away this perfectly dressed citizen. Cai looked the guy in the eye and said, "You have a nice cross, sell it to me."

Johannes could not part with the cross, because his mother gave this cross to him. Johannes loved his parents very much. Nevertheless, he realized that he could not refuse the powerful stranger. Johannes nodded. Cai pulled out a silver *thaler* and thrust it into the guy's hand.

"We have to put you in order. What is your name?"

"My name is Johannes Bauer, *Mein Herr*; I came from Innsbruck. I came in search of a job. I am a baker, sir, but I can do any other work."

"Well, well. We will start with another job, and you will bake buns, when you grow old. We have more important business for you than just baking buns."

Johannes took off his silver cross and handed it to the stranger with a bow. Cai picked Johannes's cross with two fingers and carelessly slipped it in his side pocket, meanwhile reflecting on the humanity with a sly contemptuous grin on his face, 'At first they fabulated the Crucifixion, then they idolized it, made the whole world believe in it, and now they peddle their *"Holy Crucifixes"* for the copper change near their "holy" churches.'

"Come on, Johannes, let's go, where are your belongings? Collect your things and follow me. We are going to Vienna tonight."

"*Mein Herr*, I have no belongings, this satchel is all I have."

"Actually, a man does not need anything else. Follow me."

Cai quickly walked to the carriage. There was a dense crowd of people in the street. The unemployed gathered here, there was unemployment in Switzerland, and everyone was looking for work. People migrated mainly to America to earn money.

'Poor people. All this comes from their inner voice whispering decisions to them and giving vain hope. God needs strong and intelligent souls, He does not need fools, so they toil until they grow wiser. Soon we will create a new dream and give people new hopes. In this village, it will be necessary to build a bank and decent roads, now they live like savages, having nothing. God knows how I am tired. He had turned away from me forever.'

Cai was confused in his thoughts; in addition, there that crowd completely blocked the street. Something was to be done; he was nearly behind time to meet Archibald, who punished immediately for being late. Therefore, as Cai was really afraid of being late, he shouted out loudly, "Help! They killed Karl! People, here, help!"

Everyone stared at Cai, as he yelled loudly with horror on his face, "Folks, Karl was killed, there, around the corner, there! Help!"

The crowd of people dismissed in search of the deceased Karl, while Cai quickly went to the carriage and opened the door.

"Come on, get in quickly. We do not have much time; we have to make it to a very important meeting."

The boy climbed into the carriage with his sack in hand. Cai shouted to the coachman, "Drive to *Zur Meise*, as quickly, as you can!"

The coachman took off like a bat out of hell.

Cai shouted to Johannes over the rattle of the carriage, "You're lucky to meet me! You could be born at another time and meet with Frederick... with Barbarossa! You would have sold your cross to him, and he would have burned you alive on the fire at the stake right away! Lucky you! Barbarossa, you know, was a severe man. By the way, he met with Archibald; they even had a serious project, and exceeded the plan!"

Johannes, who was not used to this style of conversation, did not understand anything at all. He believed that the stranger would give him a good job. He was ready to listen to any talk and nod his head for a plate of soup and a piece of bread.

"In the meantime, while I have a meeting with Archibald, my housemaid will wash you clean and find something to put on you. After the journey, in Vienna, we will go to the tailor and order full-fledged clothes for you."

The carriage stopped with clatter and squeak near the big house. The house was popularly called *Zur Meise*. Cai, Archibald, and all their attendants lived there temporarily. Cai pulled out a pocket watch and looked frantically at its hands, it was five minutes to six.

"I made it!"

Without paying any more attention to the guy and the servants, he uttered loudly, "Wash him clean and change his clothes!"

Cai ran at the top of his speed. He broke into the large fireplace hall panting, and saw his patron, who was bored, and did not take his eyes off the wall clock.

Archibald grinned and said, "You've made it! And I wanted to have some fun, and fry you, my beast hound. But you are lucky. What is new? Report!"

"Napoleon has lost power, and most likely, he would soon be hanged or shoved into the guillotine."

"No, everything will be fine, no one will hang him, they'll make some noise and calm down. He kept his promises, so he will remain useful for us for a long time yet. I need a theater, get down to work!"

"My lord, I promised the money to the guerillas, they want to buy weapon. I always give money for weapon. Sir, giving money for weapons is a noble deed. So I think we need to institute a bank in this house, here we will lend people money. We will create a financial center here. I plan to improve the roads here; and, what is very important, to build a railroad. Without the railroad, it is impossible to build civilization."

"Now, now, you seem to be a kind of dreamer! The hell of Jules Verne!"

"Thank you, my lord; and Sir, I found a shabby vagabond, he sold me his cross for a piece of silver. For silver. Just like Judas."

"Oh, we always need such fellows. Wash him clean, attire properly, give him a new name and put the tramp the burgomaster."

"Sir, I suppose, here we should postpone a little his admission, he is an Austrian, not a local man. I thought of making him just a rich and powerful citizen. He will serve us and everything will work, I rarely am mistaken."

"Well, well, recall how we made the emperor Napoleon Bonaparte from a soldier Buonaparte. He, too, was of Italian descent, not French."

"The time was different, and the Italians are born scammers. It was I, who found him and sent to the cadet school. And very few people know that he hated the French, and he wrote in French with mistakes, but with the help of our Radiant Lord even an ass can become an Emperor!"

"Quit insincere flattering! We have to turn this world upside down and vice versa like a pancake, so that it fries on both sides. Our task is to make life difficult for everyone, to **make** them think about **anything**, but not about what they **must** think about. We have the task to keep them here as long as possible. Napoleon will stay forever with me. He is not desired **there**, so he will always be with us."

"Sir, why do we need all these mavericks?"

"Well, it is not I who decides, it is decided without me. My task is to dunk them in their own crap, until their souls reject me completely, and they completely renounce everything and swim against the current. Such is the plan for them. Here we are trying them. They are all doomed, I know. None of them will come back. Money, fame and power, I give them everything. They trust me."

"Won't I be back either?"

"Are you not happy with me?"

"Sir, but I just had nothing else. I saw God only once; He gave me eternal life on Earth. You remember, Sir, you told me that He loved my brother, but he did not hear my prayers. You were right, Master, but I still do not know why. God hears everyone equally well. I wonder how it happened. I just approached my brother and pushed him, but that was **you**, who put the stone into my hand! It seems like that all this happened just yesterday."

"So, what is wrong with you? Do you doubt anything? You know me well; now tell me what worries you."

"Oh, nothing, my lord, I am just pondering."

"Give this guy to our monks; have them teach him writing and mathematics so that he won't go around a stupid villager. If he does not study well, cast him into the real hell, to the quarry, I am fed up with fools."

"I see, Sir, and what then?"

"And then, let him build a decent hotel here, so that we have the place to dwell. And have him collect every bit of information on visitors, so that everyone who comes to us in Zurich, and settles in this expensive hotel, needs my aid. Let us call the hotel by his new name, thus people will trust him more and will know that everything belongs to him."

"I assume it would be good to use the French name like **Baur au Lac**, meaning **Bauer on the Lake**."

"Good idea. Well done. Then choose him a wife from our maidservants so that everything will be at hand. You know, it became much easier for me to work and negotiate since the moment when THEY invented this appendage from the Adam's rib. Women are totally my best and faithful clients; I do not need to look for them, they themselves appeal to me constantly. After your mother, THEY generally mixed ordinary women and bred a kin without principles and without conscience. Women are my instrument; they serve me faithfully. Many thinkers knew the truth and claimed that women have no soul, but then under pressure they had to recognize that a woman is a sufficient creature and has a soul. St. Jerome was confident that women have no soul, that is, they are beings without a particle of God. It is easy for me to agree with him, I lead a permanent war with men, but it is very simple for me with women. Buy her a dress and beads, and she is yours forever. And with a wife and children, the man has but to surrender, he dances and sings to the tune of my flute."

Time passed, and everything went as planned. Johannes joined the majority long time ago, and, according to Archibald, was reborn in Africa. His children and the children of his children, and their grandchildren and greatgrandchildren are also Archibald's slaves, and they will not go anywhere. They will remain on the Earth for a long, long time. Forever.

Josemaria Escriva

Memories

'I met with many people in this hotel. There was the one who did not succumb; but still we got ours without him. He was the faithful servant of God, Josemaria Escriva. He was the Man of Steel. He loved and devotedly loves God, and we had no chance with him.

'They always helped him, and he dutifully served God and prayed. But, his organization, *Opus Dei*, got wet, when joined by miscellaneous pusillanimous people who were looking for their own benefit. At first, no one recognized Josemaría, but Archibald is also a Catholic, and many cardinals love him, so God sent a sign to Archibald, thus he ordered his best friend, Pope Pius XII, to recognize Escriva, and recognize his society *Opus Dei*.

'Therefore, Pius XII had but to obey, his friends fascists lost the war, and the Jews survived. And the Jews are God's chosen people, and they are vindictive.

'Consequently, Pius-XII could not get to the Holy Land in Jerusalem; his power reeled, it was necessary to strengthen his shaky position. This brat came running to the great man of our time, to the servant of God, Josemaría Escriva, and obediently aided him in everything, saving his back and his rotten soul.

'Now it is 1999, and I plan to strengthen the organization *Octopus* in Europe. They are mainly engaged in the manufacturing and transportation of drugs, but I would like arms trading to be also included in their scope. In European countries, all politicians belong to different clans, and *Octopus* is no exception. Archibald wants to establish his friend Comrade Ratzinger on the throne of Pope.

'Oh, Benedict XVI! A good choice. This Joseph Alois Ratzinger was the best friend of our Archibald, and even if Archibald was making stupid and absolutely senseless jokes, our good Benedict XVI accepted this at its face value.

'So, with the help of Alois, we will transport anything and anywhere, the Vatican mail dispatches are not subject to inspection, and thus we can, without any complications, strengthen the *Octopus* organization and involve new people.

'For a person who does not realize the full power of the Vatican mail, I will explain a math exercise. Sending one container from point A to point B costs about $ 2 million. And how many containers can be sent per day only the Devil knows. Probably, God's slave Escriva did not like that his brainchild *OpusDei* would fall into Alois Ratzinger's hands. But Josemaría did not realize that here the Earth's mundane world by the Will of the Supreme, is ruled by Lucifer, and accordingly all those who come into power are the servants of the Devil.

'Whatever on the Earth they would not call our beloved Archibald! But he never, never forced anyone to do anything. Did he force Alois to fall in love with boys or hunt homeless children in the woods with a rifle? Archibald did not force anyone; everyone made his or her own choice. A good example of this is our Josemaría, who did not succumb to the illusion of power and money, earnest Escriva had chosen God.

'Mayer Amschel said, "We do not need money, our friends print money in any quantity. So with them, and through them, we control masses. If a person believes in God and does not obey us, then we send this believer back to God. We need slaves; unquestioning slaves who will work for a piece of paper which we ourselves will print."

'The words of a genius. Yes, Archibald had been building the Tower of Babel for a considerably long time, several thousand years. But THEY didn't like it too much. I think that even now THEY don't like it; very few souls come back. I think that God will forgive us and take me away from this cursed land. Really, was the Lord God pleased that my brother Abel had been killing animals? Perhaps I stopped Abel so that he no longer killed innocent creatures? Does God require sacrifice from us literally? Does this mean that I need to slaughter an animal, which perhaps also has a soul, so that God would inhale the odor of burned meat and listen to my prayers?

Obviously not! I think that God left me on the Earth to be THEIR instrument. Abel was wrong.'

Cai woke up from his memories and returned to reality. He had been waiting for this banker for an hour and was nearly speaking aloud to himself. A man approached and addressed him and in Italian, "*Signore*, I apologize for being late; my train was held for an hour behind time. I have the tickets with me as an evidence that my delay was no fault of my own. A thousand apologies. My name is Isidoro Quatrocci and I represent the Vatican Bank."

"I know."

"Are we still waiting for someone or we can get down to business?"

"We are waiting for the American. Why are people always late? Is it so complicated to come in time? If you wish to avoid being late, then go out a day earlier, but be punctual."

"I dare say it again, *Signore*, forgive me. It will not happen anymore".

"Well, what would be the American's justification?"

"Perhaps, he was late because of the plane?"

 "He has a plane of his own and everything of his own, I will punish him, and then he will not be late anymore, but will arrive a day or two before the meeting and will be here in the hall waiting for me."

They sat opposite each other silently examining, studying each other. After an unseemly long silence, Cai inquired, "Do you have children?"

"Yes, sir, I have six children."

"Oh. So, you have but to deal with it."

Cai smiled. He understood that Isidoro would eat from his hand and implement his will. The American, whom they had been waiting for, approached them. He was in a tracksuit and sneakers.

"Hi, gentlemen, I'm David Mardisto, I represent the Rothschild Foundation."

Cai composedly nodded.

"I know. Am I distracting you from the workout, or this is your usual dress-code for a serious meeting?"

"Excuse me, but basically I always act as an investor, so I can come late, I can allow myself not come at all, I can come even naked. You need the money; I don't need anything from you."

"You, Americans, are all very presumptuous and unduly self-congratulatory. I'll tell you what. You had a green car, a truck in your childhood. You loved it and did not part with it. Your mother's name was Jessica, your father constantly abused alcohol and beat your mother, and one day, on Wednesday, he hacked her with an ax, you were 6 years old then. You have seen your mother's death. Then you were taken in an orphanage, in a poorhouse. Want me to go on? How you created your first investment company and poisoned your investor and chief with a toxic substance, polonium, and misappropriated a large amount of money? I can create for you a hell of a lot of problems, want it? Confiscation of property and prison for the beginning, you want it?"

"No."

"Kneel down and kiss my hand. I will not repeat it twice. Now!"

The American could not comprehend what was going on, but he did not want to drive Cai mad. David bent his knee and kissed Cai's hand. The people in the hall began to turn their attention to them. They have not seen anything like that yet. But Cai did not care, he fought with his anger so as not to demolish this cocky American and reduce him to dust.

"Now, David, you go, change, dress properly and sign me a check for 10 million pounds sterling."

"Yes, I'll do everything right away."

The American saw Cai from completely different point, he clearly understood that it was better not to irritate this mogul, and he had a narrow squeak.

David thought, 'Damn him, how could he know all this things about me? I have to think about how to neutralize him this Cai, let him just relax, then I will take care of him.'

 Cai looked at David and smiled.

"David, we will do it in another way. How much money do you have in your account?"

"I have 12 million dollars."

"No, David, I realize that you are stupid and arrogant. You have here in the bank bonds for 180 million euros, shares for about 3 billion euros, and a collection of diamonds. You will transfer all your property to me now; otherwise I will create such a hell for you that you can't even imagine!"

The overwhelmed American stood stunned. His thoughts were miscellaneous; nevertheless, he decided to do everything in his own way.

"Okay, Cay, as you wish, I'll give you everything. Give me at least an hour."

Cai looked at him.

"That is not all; this will be your first contribution into our business."

David was in a hurry; he dashed up to his suite, accompanied as always, by the guards from his private army. He approached his door, followed by a top-class professional bodyguard.

"Jack, come here. Gather everyone in my room."

"You got it, Boss."

David could not understand where from this bustard Cai obtained so much information. How the hell did he know facts and events, of which no one except himself had any idea? This pain-in-the-ass Cai should be eliminated immediately. Killed right here at the hotel. He poured himself some whiskey and drank it in a gulp. There was a sharp knock at the door. David opened the door. Jack and three more bodyguards stood on the threshold. All these guys were high-profile assassins, they accompanied David everywhere.

"Come on in, guys, we need to talk. Park yourselves wherever you want."

David hung the *Do Not Disturb* sign on the doorknob and closed the entrance door.

"Well, guys, we have a job to be done. I'll lay it straight for you. Downstairs in the hall there are two dudes, take care of them. Dispatch of them quietly and without any noise. I give a million euros for each, plus the performer gets a personal check for 10 million euros. Well, any questions? Can you do this job?"

"Okay, Boss, you got it."

Jack pulled out a gun. He was the leader of the team. The bodyguards were his best friends; they fought in different conflicts as mercenaries, always rescued each other, and covered one another. They were a big strong family. They went through hell together. Therefore, their friendship was impossible either to buy for money or break with money. They grabbed David by his arms and shoulders, and forced him into an armchair. David could not understand anything.

"What are you doing?"

"Shut up, you, piece of shit!"

Jack pulled out his cellphone and pressed the key.

"Mr. Cai, we are ready. Put him online? Okay."

Jack pressed his phone against David's ear.

"Well, well, hello David. You Americans are very dogmatic. How possibly can I transform you?"

"You misunderstood me, Mr. Cai. I did not wish you anything mean."

"Good. Putter-putter. It's okay."

Jack took away his phone and asked, "Mr. Cai, what's next?"

"I guess, the option number five."

"You got it, sir."

Two bulky bodyguards still kept David down. Jack grabbed David's right wrist, put a Glock into his palm, pressed the barrel against his head and shot a bullet through his right temple. It looked a common suicide. Nobody was interested in this minor accident.

Isidoro Quatrocci, sitting in the hall next to Cai and hearing a dull resound over the phone, understood right away that it was better not to upset his dangerous neighbour.

It was a good start.

"Excuse me, Mr. Cai, sir, what will we do next?"

"A mere trifle. I don't need a crowd for my plans. The dumb American did not know that all his money anyway has remained to me. Actually, I don't need money at all; it was just a theater show. Are you with me, Isidoro?"

"Yes, sir, yes, I am!"

The phone rang again. Cai began to clap upon his pockets in search of his phone. All this he did automatically. The mobile phone lay on the table. Cai grabbed the gadget.

"Yeah, go ahead. Now, Elanda, listen; unfortunately, your David died by his own hand. He accidentally shot himself with a gun. My sincere condolences. I have no time to expand on it, so I tell you briefly, send me an adequate and competent person. Find such a man, and call me. Regards to your grandfather and tell him that I am surrounded by idiots exclusively."

Without listening to the answer, Cai hung up.

"So, my dear Isidoro, I have a plan. Do you know that a prayer to God changes the physical structure of the matter? Where did you study, Izi?"

"I studied in the Vatican; I orphaned when I was 10, and was taken into an orphanage. Then I was adopted by my Catholic brothers, first I learned from them, and then at the Vatican. So what can I tell you?"

"Well, say, do you know that prayer changes the composition of blood and the structure of the matter?"

"I heard this, but there is no evidence for these statements."

"Do you know why this fact will never be published?"

"Why?"

"Because almost all institutes and laboratories and scientists completely depend on me. I respect corrupted scientists; I divide them into two groups. The first part are those who destroy their inventions; and the second group are those, who invent all kinds of unnecessary garbage. I am happy to promote thoughtless scientists who believe in Santa Claus. I am in total control of absolutely everything."

"Yes, I have come round to your way of thinking."

"Here was this jerk David, he was dumb and did not know that I, and only I, promoted the fortunes of the Rothschilds, the Rockefellers, and the Morgans. They all did well thanks to me. Here, take Rothschild, just some 200 years ago, he was a poor *pfennigless* Jew in Frankfurt, a helpless beggar. He raised 10 children, he prayed from morning to evening, and asked God for help. God sent a sign to Archibald, so he sent me to Frankfurt. Together with the Rothschilds, we built railroads and the banking system throughout Europe. He sold us his soul. God turned away from him; he became completely dependent on us. They were engaged only in blasphemy, sodomy, and incest, and we gave them power and money for it.

Same with the Rockefellers. All rich people belong to Archibald. Rothschild owes me everything; the Rothschilds financed Napoleon and financed the English who fought against him. Here the true master is Archibald; and I am his only obedient deputy.

Those people who do not keep on praying to God and do not pray with all their heart and soul, those people belong to us, and we will separate them from God. Therefore, they should be afraid of me, because God, the Creator of galaxies and of All The Existent and The Time, granted us the right to their lives. So I shit upon those earthen worms, they must fear my boot, without me they are just dirt under my soles, complete nothingness, a complete zero. You understand me?"

"I absolutely understand you, Master, how can I be useful to you?"

"You will be useful to me. Know the Rockefeller? He developed various diseases and killed nations, poisoned them with cancer and modified products so that the population of the Earth would decrease. He was very fond of Adolf Hitler, he gave him $ 11 billion, so that Hitler came to power, they had a plan to destroy the humankind and create a super race, the eugenics. Did you know that?"

"No, *Signore*, I didn't know that."

"So Isidoro, do you believe in God?"

"Obviously, *Signore* Cai, I believe very faithfully, and I earnestly pray to God."

"I see. Then why are you still talking to me? Do you recognize who I am?"

"*Si, Signore*, I know, you are Cain, the Son of Adam. I fear you, and I hope that God will forgive me my cowardice, but I fear for my children, and for my family."

"God will not forgive cowardice."

"So what should I do, how should I behave?"

"You must decide for yourself, everyone will answer to God himself, and I hope so will I. Think and give me a precise answer."

"Excuse me, Mr. Cai, can *I* ask you a question? Do *you* believe in God?"

"Listen Isidoro, you can believe in weather. I do not *believe.* I *know*, and this is a big difference. Do *you* understand the difference?"

"*Si, Signore*. I understand. Did you communicate with the Creator? Tell me please."

"I understand, you are staying with me?"

"Yes. I want to understand a lot, and I know that the price is high."

"**God does exist**, and THEY want only the very best! They do not need cowardly, weak, greedy, stupid, and envious. They require only smart, loyal and strong. And probably, if you truly repent, THEY will be able to forgive, but THEY will definitely check on. So, you will see little of good."

"I stay with you, Mr. Cai."

"Well, then let's go to my office, I'll explain to you your part of the assignments for this month. A lot of work to do. Come on, let's go. THEY are waiting for us."

Laboratory

'A shiny Rolls Royce already waited in front of the entrance. Archibald had sent it, so that we first picked up Robert from the *Bayer Company* on the way. He arrived by train, and now was waiting for us near the monument to Alfred Escher. Archibald was waiting for us to dine with him. Here is a monument to our friend Asher, according to our plan, we have built a railway and created a bank together, but stupid Alfred wanted to misappropriate everything to himself. He sold his soul to Archibald; he was a shortsighted and greedy man. We have scheduled a conversation about co-operating against humankind. Alfred Asher has built a railway in Switzerland and established a bank. He did this together with us, and then he misappropriated all the fruit for himself. And so he died, and his soul belongs to us. By our Swiss bank, Alfred financed the manufacture of weapons at his factory in 1853, these were the first 30,000 Swiss rifles designed to kill other people and wreak havoc.

'We are always happy to give a loan for weapons. But they have already worked off their way, and we decided to exterminate humankind by chemical means. Chemical weapons, modification of food and water are battling against everyone, so killing with arms is no longer relevant, and considered primitive. Here is the idea that Adolf

Hitler and the *Bayer Company* gave us. The guys from the *Bayer Company* killed by thousands at one time. This was the genius gas *Cyclone B*, the invention of a talented physician Josef Mengele. Josef Mengele cut out people's livers without any anesthesia, injected kerosene into veins, inserted colorant into people's eyes, and *Bayer* paid him for it.

'Our Archibald guaranteed a quiet life and a peaceful death to Joseph Mengele. Mengele was a demon, he liked to torture and kill people. He was a close friend of Mr. Rockefeller, who financed him, guarded him and hid him from justice. They were engaged in the breeding of the higher race, conducted the research in eugenics; seemingly a noble deed, to create a super race, but meanwhile they have been killing thousands and even millions of people. Where do you think AIDS, Ebola or cancer come from? All this is the fruitful work of the Mengele and Mr. Rockefeller's team. Like the idea to sterilize paupers and dark-skinned races. They developed diseases for entire races or nations. They studied the DNA of each race, and modified diseases and viruses for the according DNA code. Nevertheless, the problem occurred when the viruses mutated and began to kill "their own side".

'All these inhuman souls will remain with us forever. Archibald does not like Mengele and in the next thousand years, his soul in each new body will be cut, beaten, raped, burned alive and tortured in every possible way. When he will be born again, each time he will meet the severest violence, he will be nurtured with his own flesh until his vile soul comprehends the Laws. Time dimensions mean nothing to Archibald, so he can reincarnate any soul in any period of the human History; Mengele will be reborn back during the times of the Inquisition, he will be tortured, torn apart and burned alive again and again. He will undergo pain for every person to whom he brought suffering.

'The world is so deceptively arranged, that before concluding an agreement with Archibald, you need to think carefully and more than twice. But money and power blind stupid people. We drive them into debt. For a minute of glory, we take away the soul for many centuries. Is a moment of glory and all the money in the world worth eternal remaining in the everlasting shackles on the Earth? People are mostly unwise and they do not think about it.

'Now we created whole concerns, such as *Mac Donald's*, and such as *Coca-Cola*, which sell poisoned food to poor people. We made an arrangement with the tobacco industry, they add codeine to tobacco, which causes addiction and cancer. Everyone who has an attitude to those murders receives temporary benefits, so their souls belong to Archibald, who then will twist ropes of them ever after.'

The stupid Asher's monument was covered with mold, and the pigeons had befouled his bronze head with excrements. Robert Baumann, Werner Baumann's son, was already waiting for us near the green monument. He was a little confused. Cai came out personally to meet and greet him. Robert was a little scared. Cai took his suitcase and put it carefully in the trunk. Robert mostly spoke in English, but sometimes he inserted German words. Of course, Robert received excellent upbringing and education. He was polite and very reserved.

"Hello, Mr. Baumann! How do you like Zurich?"

"Zurich? Fine. Pardon me, but how shall I address you, sir?"

"Just Cai. You will know me as Cai; everyone calls me Cai in your company too, including Joseph."

"Excuse me, who is Joseph?"

"Robert, tell me how much would you like to make in a year? What is your limit?"

"I don't know, I didn't think about it yet. I have no problems with money, my grandfather left me the shares and lots of things under his will. I may not work, but just sitting around bores me, I am in a working mood."

"Robert, do you have a family, kids?"

"No, sir. I am not ready yet."

"Oh, I did not expect that you were so young."

"I am an experienced specialist; I graduated with honors from the University of Munich with a degree in chemistry and pharmaceuticals."

"Okay, we'll discuss everything at the dinner."

The limo, like a big ship, floated along the bridge and stopped at *Zur Meise*.

"So, my friends, here we are."

Cai happily jumped out of the car, ran to the door and threw them wide open, waiting for his companions.

He said in German, "Leave your belongings; they will be taken to the hotel. Come on in, let's move faster."

They entered a majestic hall, elegantly furnished with gilded antique furniture, classical paintings and medieval tapestries hung on the walls, the spacious room was established royally, sophisticatedly and expensively. There was an enormous table in the middle, covered with a burgundy tablecloth. The table was laid with antique selected porcelain tableware with exquisite handcraft pastoral vignettes, massive silver utensils, candleholders, and bronze figures. The cutlery were skillfully created by the jewelers of the previous century. It was evident that the furnishings were of the highest European level.

As a matter of fact, Archibald could turn everything into pure gold with one touch, but he did not want to attract special attention, and considered such antics childish pranks when people try to surprise others with gold. It would be primitive at the level of wild Arab sheikhs; Archibald loved modesty and respected ascetics, who surprised him by their true faith in God and their bright mind, which God bestowed upon them. But that knew no one except God. Archibald despised Arab sheikhs, he regarded them as underdeveloped savages, and considered offensive that they were all constantly praying Muslims, although doing quite the opposite to their prays. They irritated Archibald, and he waited for the command allowing him to grind into dust this Arab stupid tribe. He will burn the earth under them in such a way that there will never again grow anything alive.

Originally, Archibald's idea would be to create a deadly virus that would kill Arabs only, but not kill Jews. Jews and Arabs are of the same Semitic group descending from Abraham. The composition of the blood is like a book; by the composition of the blood, one can know everything about a person. Archibald wanted to destroy the hypocrites, while leaving alive those tribes of Bedouins and Arabs who truly obey the Laws of the Lord, believe with all their heart and soul, and act nobly. Archibald did not want to irritate the Creator.

He knew that by the composition of the blood he would be able to distinguish the righteous person from a dumb animal. Archibald knew that God would not be very upset if the worst of the Arab tribes died off. He did not want to simply defeat the Arab ignorance with his power; he wanted them to kill each other. Archibald wanted to prove once again to his Creator all the idiocy of humankind. He needed scientists, the best team of chemists and biochemists, and the best laboratory. And Archibald thought of nothing better than to turn to his old and trusted friends, namely, the *Bayer Company*, who loved to do experiments on people.

'The German will like my idea,' Archibald thought.

"Hello my friends, please, accommodate yourselves."

Cai immediately responded to the words of his master and showed everyone his place.

"We are only four, and the place immediately became scarce," Archibald joyfully chattered.

Isidoro was afraid even to look at Archibald, knowing perfectly well, who was before him. But Robert, like any German, was still waiting for the most important thing, he would not believe that his peer could organize such a thing. Germans are a little stupid in terms of assessing other people. The root of their stupidity is a sincere belief that they are the smartest, and that they can calculate absolutely anyone and any life situation with a mathematical equation.

Archibald glanced at Robert and said, "Sit down on your seat; or are you waiting for someone else?"

Overwhelmed Robert sat down on his chair and thought, 'Why does he talk to me like that? Do I deserve such a harsh attitude?'

"I say Robert, do you know who I am?"

"I have not been introduced to you yet, *Mein Herr*."

"I am Archibald."

"Oh, *Herr* Archibald, forgive me my carelessness. I just imagined you different."

"How different? A woman?"

"*Nein, Mein Herr*, older. Much older."

"I **am** much older than you and **even older** than your *Bayer Company*."

"*Herr* Archibald, forgive my ignorance, but older than *Bayer*, how shall I understand it? I suppose, you are just joking?"

"Joking, dear Robert, just joking. Therefore, I need to discuss with you the project that my deputy Cai started. I need the best chemists and biochemists for blood testing. Have you read the project that Cai sent you?"

"Yes. It is necessary to determine the difference between people according to the testimony of blood test results. Investigate the blood of people and DNA. Search for differences between races and lifestyles."

"Yes, and I also need to create in the laboratory an isotope of gold that will instantly develop cancer in a person."

"I think that would be impossible, *Mein Herr*. Our company does not develop substances that harm humankind."

"Robert, this baloney you will be pushing to your students at lectures, not me. You memorize what I need, otherwise you will be fired from the company like a cork from a champagne bottle, and even your dad will not help. Then, I will take care of the inheritance of your grandfather, who killed people together with Mengele. All legally, through the court, we will make you guilty of the death of thousands of people, and you will give everything to the last *pfennig* for the compensation. I will make you a beggar; you will live in a cardboard box in a back street, and eat from the garbage can. I fully guarantee you that. Are we clear?"

"Dear *Herr* Archibald, are you threatening me?"

"Listen, you jerk, gather up your stuff and get the hell out of the city! One more human rights defender here! I am breaking any relationship with you and *Bayer*, you will see how soon you all will end up in the garbage can, I will check on to it personally," Cai said.

"Why so radically, *Herr* Cai, my grandfather told me a lot about you, and I do not want to break off business relations with you; I am just scared of the consequences. Grandpa told me how you saved our company and put us back on feet. I do not want to put everyone in jeopardy. *Herr* Archibald, forgive me for my stupid question, I was just afraid of the consequences."

Cai, looking straight in the eye of the astonished chemist, distinctly said in German, "So, henceforth, first think twice, and then formulate a question or a sentence. Are we clear?"

The German nodded dumbly.

Archibald continued the clarification, "There will be no consequences, I solve such questions here. You will not comprehend; I am the court, and for you, I am the highest authority. Clear?"

"I completely understand you, *Herr* Archibald, so we will create a closed type laboratory, strictly secret, in the museum, near our factory, the locations will be connected by underground tunnels, but that will be a very expensive enterprise in the money aspect. We will have to double our scientists' salary for their silence. This is approximately 35 million euros for the creation of an autonomous laboratory plus approximately 16 million euros per year for the maintenance and development of new chemical agents. I figured it out approximately, to a minimum. It can pull more."

"I don't care how much it costs. The main thing is that you never deceive me and never doubt my abilities."

Archibald's eyes were burning with rage at the stupid German.

"*Herr* Archibald, I am not going to deceive you, *Mein Herr*. I have never deceived anyone in my life and neve stole anything. I do not need anything anybody else's."

"Well, now I think that our dear friend Isidoro supports us and is completely ready to finance our wonderful project. Do you represent the Vatican? Actually, the Arabs always bothered you. Here, now you can get even with them for Jerusalem. After the launch of our virus, crowds of thoughtless people will immediately arrive in the Vatican in search of salvation. Therefore, in addition, you will earn again, you will sell candles and pardon sins to your sheep, and the stupid herd will again donate money to you."

"Khmm, khmm... Oh, please give me some water... I got my throat dry..."

"Isidoro, what is the matter with you?"

A servant quickly entered the hall with a glass of water and set it in front of Isidoro. Isidoro grabbed a glass with both hands and drank it to the bottom.

"Yes, my dear *Signori*, our bank is ready to cooperate with you on any conditions, even if it goes to the detriment of the entire Vatican. As for me, I completely trust you and your actions, so in the Vatican's name I declare that we are ready to finance and give the necessary sums of money for the development of science without any conditions."

"Oh, science! I really like the word **science**! For example, the development of the *Cyclone B* gas, this is **pure science**, otherwise you cannot say. Developed a gas to exterminate their own kind. Yes. This is the case, true and pure science. We will now also contribute to **pure science**; we will develop a virus that will kill millions. This is the science in action. After they start to breathe their last breath, I am going to demand a Nobel Prize for me!"

"*Herr* Archibald, it would be better to receive the Nobel Prize now, otherwise they will all die from our virus and there will be no members of the Nobel Prize Committee left to give you a well-deserved award."

"That is true, the world consists mostly of ugly and corrupt villains, and those who are really interesting to me, THEY take to THEMSELVES. I have only outcasts left. Okay, enough about the sad. Now, let them bring in the delicious food! Let the banquet commence!"

Archibald clapped his hands, and the whole army of servants with trays above their heads entered the dining hall under the sounds of classic music. There were exquisite dishes from all over the world; it was the first part only, a cold snack and wine. The wines were not ordinary, each bottle had witnessed a sinful fall at a different time, the owners of these bottles had long been lodging in the cemetery, and their souls were chained to rotting bodies. Oh, THEY are able of everything! Mussolini loved red wine; it reminded him of human blood. Thus, there was the complete wine collection on the table that once belonged to Benito Mussolini.

Isidoro had understood everything a long time ago, but the German chemist was in great shock. The Radiant can embellish the most dreadful things. The German chose power and money, and direct participation in the massacres, he did not want to change his fate, and become a pauper, though a sinless person. **Did Archibald *force* him to agree?**

Seraphim

After the luxurious banquet, Cai drove his guests to the hotel. Cai has booked the best suite at the *Baur au Lac Hotel* for everyone. Cai settled Robert and Isidoro at the hotel, then returned to Archibald.

Archibald was sitting near the fireplace. Fire is our element. Cai walked in without a word and lodged in a large leather chair.

"When you look at the fire, all your thoughts disappear, as if the fire is consuming everything."

"The problem is, that we always have everything the same, every day everything is the same; yesterday I visited an Egyptian Pharaoh and caught myself on thinking that people do not change at all. They are born and reborn and in every new life, they constantly make the same old mistakes. They are all the same, primitive creatures, arrogant, stupid, and ungrateful."

"Yes, Master, but are there any exceptions?"

"There are exceptions. I will have him brought to us. We will study him."

"It is necessary to make it in time because what if suddenly, THEY will decide to take him to THEMSELVES, so what then?"

"I will be the first to know when THEY decide to summon him. So Cai, the simplest to deal with is all that you can acquire for money. Any problem that is solved for money means expenses. But Seraphim means a problem not to solve for money, it would be improper to offend him, and it is impossible to force him to something; we must convince him in some decent way to participate in our project. It would be not very easy, he is devoted to the Lord God, and God has endowed him with a subtle and enlightened mind, so that we will not succeed in deceiving him. He is the only one among people who instantly distinguishes lies from truth and nearly reads people's minds. For all this, he sincerely prayed God, and He made Seraphim, as you can put it, almost a Superman. A powerful and invincible servant of the Lord God transformed himself from a hard-core brute and murderer. I have tried nearly every trick on him already; he scents me for miles. Therefore, Cai, ponder well how to arrange everything so that he would trust you and start talking to you."

"I understand, sir; so tomorrow I fly to Moscow. See you later, Messire. We will meet not too soon."

"Everything will happen faster than you can think."

Cai went back to the hotel. He just wanted to remain alone in silence, emotionally detached from the disturbing thought of Seraphim. Why did the Lord God bring this Seraphim closer to THEM, and distanced him?

'He had committed much more sins then I had, and I, as it were, due to a misunderstanding, merely knocked my brother on his head with a stone, and I repent every day and speak with God every night, but THEY remain silent. This rogue shot people with a machine gun, robbed banks, violated all existing laws; nevertheless, THEY have forgiven this mobster's crimes, and took him closer to THEMSELVES.

And now, he is a devotee, I have to look for an approach to him. Why not do, as he used to do, in broad daylight gun-butt him on the mug, tie him up, shove in the trunk of the car, and bring to the laboratory? Alas, no, it is impossible, he, you see, has become a saint, and I must beg him and persuade him. Should I, I, who was one of the first man, the son of Adam, seek a common language with some kind of a beast?'

He was so upset he could cry. Scarce tears wetted Cai's stern and angry face, he was distressed, he talked to God every evening, but received no answer. Archibald knew this, and in the depths of his mind, he completely agreed with Cai. The powerful creatures of the Lord God always bear a great burden of responsibility. From time immemorial, Cai did not know what slumber is, he had already forgotten that there is a state other than being awake. If a common man sleeps half of his life, then according to the result, he actually lives half of his life; one cannot consider life experience the time, when a person sleeps. A dream is a gift from God; only those acceptable before God are sleeping. God takes away sleep from for all unworthy people, so they have to take various medications to drug themselves into sleep. Although this is not sleeping, but immersion into a dark oblivion. God sends beautiful and sweet dreams only to worthy people. God did not give sleep to Cai. Cai took a hot bath and went to his fresh and clean bed, lying prone and still with his eyes closed.

Meanwhile, Isidoro approached Robert Baumann's suite. Robert talked on Skype with his girlfriend from Munich. Isidoro had no desire just to talk; he wished to turn back time, because his heart anticipated a trouble, a very grave disaster.

Isidoro knocked hard on the door and shouted, "Open up, this is Isidoro, we need to talk."

"Right away, give me just a minute!"

Robert turned back to his laptop to say goodbye to his girlfriend. Then he put on his bathrobe and headed for the door.

"What do you want Isidoro? I'm already having my rest and I have no desire to discuss anything with you."

"You should have. Besides, I intend to discuss with you our future. Personally, I am very scared, and it may be too late to alter our decisions, perhaps it will cost us our lives, but I cannot live with this anymore. We all will be accomplices in the massacres, and we will be responsible for this before God. Do you comprehend what mess we got into?"

"How can personally I help you? Everyone must define his own future. I have already decided my own. I have no other choice; they will destroy my life and the whole company. They have in their hands all the main shareholders of the company; and if they all withdraw their capital, then they will grind our mighty company into dust. I have already pondered everything."

"It's not a question of money. Do you understand **WHO** Archibald is?"

"Archibald is a very influential businessman."

"Do you hear what you are saying? Archibald is the real Devil! **We made a deal with the Devil himself!** God will not forgive us this!"

"Dear Isidoro, I do not believe in God. Only losers constantly hide behind God so that they can lump their blames and faults on somebody else. **God does not exist**."

"O Lord, Robert, you really do not believe in God? Then what happens after death? What will happen to us, what do you think?"

"We will die and that's all. However, that will be not too soon."

"Dear Robert, I have to prove you that God exists, so that you understand that we have been recently talking to Lucifer himself."

"Well, I quite understand you, this is your job in the Vatican to frighten the poor and stupid with Satan; but I, and all my relatives, no longer believe in Santa Claus and other fairy tales. I understand that they pay you a lot of money for it, and all those idiots make donations every day to make it easier for you to fight the Devil and other spooky Evil."

"Good. I understand that we are getting with our conversation nowhere. Now I will ask you a simple question. Cai knew your grandfather, who told you a lot about Cai and how Cai saved your company after the WWII. Was your grandfather 98 years old? Then how old is Cai? Seemingly, he looks at most forty-five."

"It is possible that he developed some drug that slows down the aging process of a person and stopped this process. Grandpa told me that they had been developing cosmetics for rejuvenation. He spoke about the secret elixir of the Egyptian god Ra, who gives youth and eternal life on the Earth. Perhaps he succeeded and thus remained young."

"What a fool you are Robert! Total *douche*! Ra is not an Egyptian god, but radium! Radium is a radioactive substance, from which they made expensive cosmetics so that people suffer from cancer and infertility. They made radioactive toys for kids. Then, they invented a radioactive drinking water container. Surf the Internet; everyone knows that. It was their program for the mass destruction of the population, similar to the one, that we are going to develop with you. Here is your Egyptian god Ra. Just as *Coca-Cola* had 9 milligrams of cocaine in each bottle, and everyone drank it, both adults and children. A miracle drink made of cocaine, and cocaine is not excreted from the DNA during the next 15-20 years. Therefore, all these miracles of health and vigor hide in them slow death for us and our children. Then they also came up with the idea that *Philip Maurice's* cigarettes help pregnant women, and doctors prescribed these cigarettes to mothers-to-be. This information is available to everyone on the Internet, in the archives, but is not interesting to anyone. How many people did these inventions kill? How many strains of all the flu viruses and Ebola epidemics did they produce? We do not know. Nevertheless, this Archibald *is* the Devil. Only God can save us. The God you do not believe in."

"Yes, I do not believe in God and I do not think that we have any problems. Archibald said that he would solve all the problems. Moreover, I will require a written contract from him, and then there would be no escape for him. I am afraid of nothing. I have very good lawyers."

"Okay, I understand you. Sorry to disturb you at such a late time."

Isidoro went out into the hallway and realized that he had made a grave mistake, sharing his fears with the German moron. Because everything, absolutely everything that we say aloud, Lucifer hears, then he acts accordingly.

In counted seconds, the phone rang in Isidoro's pocket. Isidoro felt that the conversation would be stern.

"This is Cai. What is the problem with you? My intuition tells me that there you are telling all sorts of nasty things about us. Is that good?"

"Dear Mr. Cai, I know who you are and I fear you. I am aware of the whole situation, and I am aware of my position. I understand that I made a contract with Lucifer himself and there is no turning back. I am a coward. And cowardice is certainly the most ignoble human vice. God does not need cowards."

"Listen, I would be happy to see God myself, but everything is in its time. I did what I did, and Lucifer helped me to withstand, because I was about to commit another sin. God probes each of us. You have nothing to fear, there is no sin behind you yet."

"You know that this is not quite so. And you know perfectly well in what situation I am. I estrange myself and I am ready to die, but I will not work with you. I will contact Cardinal Alberto right away and pass him all the documents."

"Fine, Isidoro; then what will you do?"

"I will go to the monastery, and I will pray to God until the end of my days."

"This will not save you; God will bring you back to this situation anyway, and you will have to decide for yourself."

"I have made a decision now, I am leaving, and no one will return me back to you."

"Isidoro, remember, your soul is in my pocket. And even if you leave, I will do with you absolutely everything I want anyway. In any case, you will not live in peace, I promise. Archibald will install your soul into the body of his dog and you will be a dog for a long time. Then we will install you in the body of a laboratory frog, and they will experiment on you without anesthesia, you will die of pain several times a day. You have no choice. I am not deceiving you."

"There always is an exit from any situation. My head was clouded when I took this long spoon that sups with the Devil and was afraid to leave. But now, I don't care. Therefore, Cai, I wish you good luck. So long."

Isidoro threw the phone against the marble floor with all his strength, and the gadget shattered into small fragments. He understood that his whole life went to hell like this phone.

Isidoro yelled at the top of his lungs, "*Maladetto*! Son of a bitch! What to do? WHAT AN IDIOT I AM!!!"

Isidoro ascended to his suite and turned on a secluded video connection with the Vatican. He dialed the subscriber Cardinal Alberto. The Cardinal did not get in touch, so Isidoro switched to his assistant, Santuccio. Santuccio immediately picked up the call.

"*Pronto*, I'm listening to you, *Signore* Isidoro!"

"Santuccio! Do you believe in God?"

"Absolutely, with all my heart, *Vostra Eminenza.*!"

"Bless you, Santuccio! Now, bring your Holy Bible and put your right hand on the Bible. Accept Our Lord God the Highest Creator as your Witness. And everything that you say will be true, and everything that you promise me, you will do, even if you are threatened with death."

"*Si, Vostra Eminenza*, I solemnly swear!"

"*Perfetto*. Put your right hand on your Bible so that I see it. *Bene*. Listen. I will send you all the access codes to my accounts by coded E-mail, in the same message I will write everything what should be done with the money. I will leave all my property to the *Opus Dei* under your management. I will write letters and leave a video message for the cardinals and separately for Cardinal Alberto. I am fine; I merely have to leave the organization. I will inform them that you should occupy my present position. In addition, I immediately advise you, beware of the Devil, because he is always near us. I say farewell to you, dear Santuccio. *Buona fortuna*! Good luck! God is with us!"

Isidoro killed the connection and began to record a video message to the cardinals, giving them the knowledge that he voluntarily left this life. He did not explain the reason, and did not indicate it in his E-mail. He removed the crucifix from his neck, and a small pill popped up from the secret hole. This pill was called the "*Judgment of God*." It is funny, but this transport to God always worked flawlessly. Everyone knows that killing oneself is a grave and unpardonable sin, but who knows exactly that God would punish for it? Isidoro knew that he had plenty of reasons. He made a mistake and wanted to punish himself for his fault and cowardice. In the letters he allocated his assets into various trustworthy funds. He bequeathed his possessions to orphans and impoverished people, and the elderly, who were left unattended. In his letter, he pointed out the only condition: to help true believers only. He transferred a million euros to the publishing house for printing the Bible and books of devotion. Also Isidoro ordered to pay regularly additional funds to support the *Maltese* and *Red Cross*.

'God forgive. God forgive. God forgive me!'

He put the pill in his mouth and swallowed it. Less than in a minute, his ears popped, then his arms and hands turned cold, like marble. He wanted to lie down on the sofa, but his legs did not obey, the poison had an immediate effect. He collapsed on a glass coffee table. The table shattered into pieces with a rattle. Isidoro lay prone, his body completely numb; it was an instant almost painless death. His eyes did not blink, but the consciousness was clear and his soul still remained in the body. Isidoro could not move. Suddenly, a fragrance of cinnamon and vanilla filled the room. Isidoro saw no one; a monotonous sound buzzed in his ears. Unexpectedly, someone took him by the legs and dragged him to the sofa, grabbed him by the collar, picked up from the floor, and threw his body on the sofa.

"Well, well, hello, weirdo!"

A beautiful young girl was bending over Isidoro. A longhaired dark-eyed brunette. She was casually dressed in a bleached denim jacket and jeans, her mountain boots with thick soles were dirty. Isidoro wanted to say something, but his body was dead and no longer obeyed him. The beauty suited herself opposite the deceased in a cozy armchair and continued, "So, Isidoro. What do you come up with? Huh, Isidoro? What crap did you gobble? Kind of a heart stopper? Effective drug. In short, today you did not succeed. You are not forgiven, but do not you try this trick anymore. You have to live and help other people turn to God. You do not need to fear the Devil, for God created him as THEIR assistant, so that he would select worthy souls. He remotes only the weak and the stupid. You need not be afraid of Lucifer, you know the truth, and therefore it is impossible to deceive you. Come back to him and work, he himself will leave you alone. Now get some sleep, rest and take to your job tomorrow."

Isidoro opened his eyes, he lay on the sofa, fully dressed, and his head was splitting. It was half past seven. The sky was gray, the sun tried in vain to shine through thick dark clouds. Isidoro recalled the previous day, and realized that this was not a dream. He went to the table; a thick, silver chain with the crucifix lay on the table and the secret lid was open. Isidoro took the venom and survived. Was this not an evidence of God? Isidoro fell to his knees and began to pray, tears flowed down his cheeks in a flood. God gave him a chance. Isidoro prayed earnestly, then got up, looked at the ceiling and said aloud, "Thank You, O Lord! Thank You for all!"

Isidoro went to the bathroom and took a hot shower; he wanted to wash off the yesterday. After the intensive water procedures, he put on new clothes, which he had prepared for the conference. After all this, he knelt again and continued to pray and thank God for loving-kindness. There was a knock at the door. Then he heard Cai's low voice, "Hey, Vatican, open up!"

Isidoro opened the door.

"ALOHA, Son of Adam. What brings you here? We have an appointment at twelve; anything happened?"

"You seem to have been replaced, Isidoro, you had surprised me yesterday."

"Yesterday I felt unwell, and today we are fine."

"Who are those 'we'?"

"I and my friend Cardinal Alberto."

"Clear, I am glad you are with us. I need you to sign me a check."

"For what sum?"

"Fifty thousand euros, to begin with."

"For what purpose?"

"I have to find some man in Russia. Money is needed for travel expenses."

"Clear. And when do you take off?"

"Tonight, to Moscow."

"Good luck. Hope your plane will not crash."

"You know that I am marked, and cannot count on such a luck."

Isidoro, humming *Ave Maria* under his breath, pulled out his briefcase. It was his favorite old leather briefcase; he found it in the archives of the Vatican. Isidoro restored the portfolio and kept the most important documents in it. The checkbook of the Vatican Bank could bear any imaginary amount. Isidoro inserted the number in the filled check and passed it to Cai's hand, with the words, "Hard to imagine that the richest man on this sinful Earth does not have travel money."

"It is not a question of money, but of your presence and participation."

"Actually I don't care, until recently, I was very deeply worried and pondered a lot. That led me to nothing good, for all is the Will of the Lord God."

"But you really have changed, what had happened to you?"

"I learned to fly!"

"I'm seriously asking you! What's up, Isidoro?"

"Nothing, I got all the answers, that's all."

"It is interesting, that I know nothing about this."

"This is beyond your competence, my dear friend."

"Oh, clear! You had a dream and an angel appeared?"

"Yes, so it was."

"Why I cannot see your thoughts?"

"Because there are no thoughts. Yes, I did have a dream. So, I wish you success in your journey."

"If I may ask you, would you please not sing this song in my presence."

"Does *Ave Maria* annoy you? Why?"

"Because I get the impression that you are unwell."

"Oh, no, I feel great, I understand you, I will not sing. Wish you a happy journey."

Isidoro walked to the front door and defiantly opened the door, gesturing to the hallway.

"See you soon, Mr. Vatican."

Cai went out into the hallway. Isidoro slammed the door shut.

"Go with God," Isidoro said.

Then with a broad smile, he began to sing *Ave Maria* at the top of his voice. Never in his life was he in such a mood and a surge of strength.

Cai hurried to the bank, and then to the airport, he wanted to buy tickets at the airport because he did not really trust the online Internet booking. The operator in the bank instantaneously recognized Cai and hastily rushed to fetch the main manager. Usually the bank employees are sluggish and slow, like sleepy flies, but when Cai appeared, everyone revived and began to fuss about.

They immediately ushered Cai to the office for VIP customers, where his favorite steaming hot espresso with Swiss chocolate was already waiting for him on the table. Cai thought that *Lindt's* chocolate is the most delicious in the world, and thus they will stay here for a long time too.

The manager came running. He was always smiling like all bankers, like top-class geishas; they have delicate skin, well-groomed hands; they are always dressed exquisitely and with immaculate gusto. They are apt to anything for the sake of money. Bankers are a closed caste who pass down their dark secrets from generation to generation; they do not allow anyone to intrude from the outside. They suck our blood. We ourselves feed this pure evil from our hand.

Thus, Rothschild created the banking system, and did not let anyone into his circle, he married his son to his daughter, he was ready to marry himself, just so as not to let in people from the outside. So, why? You ask, why? Because it is the best profession in the world, not anything better simply exists. This is the coolest profession. In fact, everyone in the world earns money, someone bakes bread, someone works in the factory, someone other steals and robs, and, as a result, everyone, absolutely everyone wants to bring their hard-earned money to you and give it to you. What are those politicians, presidents in comparison – pure suckers! Bankers mean money every second and always. Presidents come to the bank, not the other way around. Once there was a smart alec, who decided to manage the banks, a certain Kennedy, so he was immediately shot down.

This is how banks work; they are the best invention of Archibald. Thus, Mayer Amschel Rothschild signed a contract with Archibald, and very successfully.

'Now, here comes this banker, the son of the manager, a complete scoundrel and scum, he is ready to lick my shoes because he knows that I am fabulously rich.'

"How can I help you, Mr. Cai?"

"Hello, please transfer to my account and issue me a *Centurion* bank card and one hundred thousand euro in cash."

"Excuse me, sir; we cannot issue *Centurion* immediately, only after 10 working days after the application."

"I am going to Russia, if I need money, what should I do then?"

"You do not need to worry, Mr. Cai. I will give you traveler's checks and business cards of our direct partners who will be always ready to help you."

"I assume you have partners in every country?"

"Yes, sir, in every country where there is money."

Cai lounged in a leather armchair and no longer wanted to hurry anywhere. The coffee was delicious, the chocolate melted in his mouth and he thought that everything, absolutely everything that he sees, belongs to him. This manager did not comprehend the whole truth, and Cai was not going to enlighten him. Cai decided to find out what this banker was eager to accept in order to satisfy the client.

"Can I call you on your personal number?"

"Obviously, sir, I already gave you my business card with my personal phone that works around the clock."

"And if I ask you to do something for me?"

"Mr. Cai, I am always ready to help you."

"Can you go to the church and dump a pile there?"

"No, sir, unfortunately, no, I can't do that."

"Why? What's stopping you?"

"Excuse me, sir; this is madness and disgrace."

"Yes, but what can you tell about Mr. Goldstein?"

"Mr. Goldstein is our most important investor and co-owner of the bank."

"I am Samuel Goldstein. I am the full owner of this bank, only your father knows this and no one else."

"It is clear, sir. It is very sad."

"Why is it sad?"

"Will I have to dump piles in the church regularly, according to your wishes?"

"No, just once."

"Why do you demand this? I do not understand."

"I must understand if you are able to sacrifice yourself for my sake."

"Then what happens after I complete your assignment? Will there be a new delusional request, or will it be an order?"

"Everything is voluntary. I am not forcing you to anything."

"Then I quit if you are serious, sir."

"Are you a believer?"

"No, sir, I am just a well-educated person and I am not ready to perform such absurd tasks."

"I understand. Your decision is correct. We will talk again when I get back. So far it was our acquaintance, although I know everything about you, you grew up before my eyes. You are Daniel; a native of Switzerland, married, you have one child, your son's name is Rachiel."

Daniel's eyes became round, he was overwhelmed.

"I understand, sir, that my father told you that?"

"Yes. He told me that you behaved badly; you were caught on money laundering for the Colombian cartel. I hushed up this thing, along with your father. You were tempted by money, and now you are telling me about the decent upbringing?"

"Sir, I didn't do that for money, I want to be independent of my family. Can you understand me, sir?"

"It cost us almost 25 million euros, and how much did you make with the Colombians? Your father was crawling on his knees; he was ready to do anything to get you out of this case and remove any suspicions from you."

"I did not know it, sir."

"Okay, now you'll know. I'm going to Russia; do not do any more stupid things."

"I understand you, sir. Thank you, sir I did not know that you liberated me of this calamity."

"Live quietly and keep both eyes wide open. I will contact you."

Cai collected cash and travelers checks and tucked them into his pocket. He had to buy tickets and take in the situation by the time. Life was boring for Cai, like a tedious TV series. He knew everything about people, he could feel and read everyone.

Common people are all the same, they are divided into four castes, the first are bums, they do not need anything and live like stray dogs, thinking for one day only.

The second caste are slaves who work from morning till evening, like squirrels who turn the wheel until they die, they have no time to think about God and about the righteous life. They think about how to buy grub and how to find a better salary to buy household trifles. This is an inglorious caste, they are born unnoticeable, and die unnoticeable, and no one considers them.

The third caste are spiders, these are predators, who know a lot about God; many of them believe in God, but they do not live by the generally accepted rules. They never stop to lie, rob, and kill. Very often, they achieve what they want in any way. They are difficult to predict, they are like venomous animals, from which you can expect absolutely everything. Most of these people are Archibald's best friends, they are Cai's children, these people are outlaws, they do not obey the laws, and Archibald is happy to help them.

The fourth caste are philosophers, pundits, they are not interested in material things, they study the nature of things, reflect on the cosmos and on eternal life. They are like dandelions, there is no use of them, and no harm either. They are very far from God, because they want to analyze the presence of God logically and calculate

THEM using a formula or seeing THEM through a telescope. This category of people does not interest Cai at all; they are colorless and tasteless to him.

But the fifth type is not a caste, they are *"the sons of Abraham"*. These people can be counted on one hand. They know the truth and they are special people who are not afraid of anyone or anything but God. For them, God is the meaning of life.

They are like people who are standing at a bus stop and waiting for their bus, they are absolutely not interested in anything. They do not go into politics, they do not need money, they think about God only, and God sends them everything they need to wait for their time. God gifted them an enlightened mind and willpower. All friends and family have renounced them. They are completely different, and they have different interests. Cai has to communicate regularly with these people. He knows them all; God chose them. They are a chosen tribe, the untouchables. God has endowed them with intelligence and power, they have such energy that they can influence any events and processes. However, they never interfere. They are indifferent to other people, because, they know the truth. One of this type was Seraphim. Cai went to meet Seraphim.

He had to meet in Moscow a certain priest who probably knew the whereabouts of Seraphim. The church did not recognize Seraphim, for them he was just an ordinary hermit. They did not attach any importance to him. God created this theater and everyone had to perform his part.

Cai left the bank, the wind hit him in the face and he breathed in fresh air. A *Rolls Royce Phantom* stood before the entrance; it was a very comfortable and very fast car. Cai sat in the back seat and addressed his driver and friend Jack, "Drive to the airport, I will buy tickets and then back home, I'll pick up the most necessary things."

"Okay, you got it, Boss."

Jack was not fond of talking a lot, he was a mercenary, and, after all the military campaigns, had no heart, no soul. Jack was a faithful and devoted man. The state used him and threw out into the street. Jack turned out to be unemployed and homeless. Cai gave him everything he wanted. Jack, in gratitude, served him faithfully, and executed any order.

"Did this Elanda call you?"

"Yes, she did."

"What did you tell her?"

"Suicide. That's all."

"Well done. She said whom will they send?"

"Some woman, kind of a secretary, she will come and sign everything."

"Wonderful. If she calls you again, tell her that I will talk with a blood relative of the Rothschild family only. Only with them. They will send me now another inadequate employee. If there is a suicide, only bloodline matters, so that they pay us. Does she trust you?"

"Yes, they think I work for them. They are bankers; they think that absolutely everything can be bought for money."

"That's fine, we need such kind. They themselves prolong their life on the Earth. Think, who came up with the edible gold? This is my invention, so that eventually they would eat tar. They pay money for profligacy, this is their first sin, then they get sick, and start treating themselves with illegal methods, they pay a lot of money, this is the second sin, they leave us their bastards, who will then continue to commit their sins. They are on fire. They are here forever, for a couple of years of careless life, they give us their souls forever. We will forge these souls like iron. Into the fire, and then under the sledgehammer, and again into the fire, heating to white, and then again for a long time under the sledgehammer, until we shape them. After that, we will form them and polish for a long time. Then, when we carve the form, and this soul will endure all the torments, we will again give it power and money, and we will sign a blood contract with them, and again fire and a sledgehammer. That is such a thousand year cycle for a couple of years of a rich and carefree life.

"Archibald hates people and does the right thing. I hate them too, although I am one of the first, and THEY rejected me because I am defective. I want to be the first, although I have no right to it. Moreover, these scum, how can they be compared with me? Buying themselves edible gold! That is how sick they are! They want to stand out in front of the others, they buy themselves wine for half a million dollars a bottle! This is vinegar! How can one pay half a million dollars for a bottle of vinegar? They should rather spend this money to save themselves! For every beggar whom they feed now, they will feed themselves in the future. They do not know the truth, that by helping others, they save themselves. They can build an ark for themselves with good deeds. Nevertheless, they do not do so, for they are very greedy. Instead of reducing hell for themselves, they extend it for centuries. They do not understand the simple rule,

<u>Lighting the way for others, you light the way for yourself!</u>

"That rule they will never comprehend. They will arrange standing buffets, drink vinegar for a million dollars, devour edible gold, actually metal, which brings harm in this life and in the next. I also want to invent edible stones, somewhat like 'Swarovski edible stones'. Now, that is their fate and their souls, let them do what they want."

"Yes, Master, what if I did not learn your wisdom in time and now am in trouble? How can I fix this?"

"It's like in school, you missed lessons and you were left for the next year!"

"I missed not only a year, but the whole school. We have arrived."

"Wait for me here. It won't be long. Then to the airport and that is all, you are free."

"Mr. Cai, can I go with you?"

"No, you'd rather wait for the representative of the house of Rothschild."

"But they think as I work for them, I will be with you, and inform them on you."

"Will you fink on me?"

"Yes, new options. Con them."

"Okay, then, while I collect my things, go to your place, get yours. And be right back here. We have little time. And we should buy a ticket for you."

"Yes, sir!"

Cai easily pushed *Rolls-Royce's* door and it closed by itself. He went to his room; his belongings were collected. He dialed the internal telephone number of the hotel, *"Halo, schicken Sie bitte zu mir den Kofferträger."*

He was too lazy to carry the suitcase and the bag himself. He called a porter who would do everything for free. Many services were free, but Cai still gave money to people who wanted to live honestly and did not want to step on other peoples' heads. Cai knew the price of each person and knew exactly how long and how everyone would live, but did not know when his own time would come. There was a delicate knock at the door.

"Yes, come in."

A man in a nice uniform entered the room. The whole hotel staff was dressed this way. The door attendant was an elderly man with very sad eyes, but he managed a broad smile and asked, "Monsieur, how can I help you?"

Cain looked at the porter and felt a heartache.

"Excuse me, what is your name?"

"Alberto Giovannini, Monsieur".

"Sit down, Alberto."

"Sorry Monsieur, I am not allowed. If someone sees me sitting, they will fire me right away."

"No one will fire you, this is my hotel. Rather the sky will fall than you get fired. Do you understand?"

"Yes, Monsieur, it is quite possible, but I see you for the first time and cannot risk my work."

"Okay, if you want to stand, then stand. Do you believe in God?"

Alberto had tears in his eyes, his face slightly contorted, but he held back. Alberto forced a smile and squeezed out of himself, "Yes, Monsieur, I devotedly believe in God."

"That's the right way you do it. You prayed a lot lately. Have you had any grief?"

"This is personal, Monsieur, and I would rather not talk about it."

"You should not tell, I know everything myself. Your wife has been ill with cancer for the third year and I know that you sold all the property for her sake, you live in a hotel now and give all your salary to your health insurance."

Alberto burst into crying, tears poured out in a flood, and he could no longer hold back. He sat down on the sofa and covered his face with his hands. He could not speak. Cain felt his pain. God forgave Alberto and allowed Cain to support him.

"Look, don't cry anymore. God hears your prayers. God forgives you, but do not forget to pray, and teach your wife. Pray to God, and prayer will heal her. Look, cancer is treated with grass that grows everywhere on the street. This grass is dandelion, namely dandelion juice. Your Augustine has the stomach cancer, doesn't she?"

"How do you know my wife's name, Monsieur?"

"Remember my prescription and do as I tell you. For three days, she should neither drink anything nor eat anything. Then for three days in a row, give her only dandelion juice and the illness will go away. And pray, pray constantly to God and teach your wife to pray. Thus, you will be saved. Quit your job and get busy with your wife only. And so that no one distracts you, you must take her home from the hospital. I'll give you some money so that you can buy back your house and live in peace."

Cain pulled out a checkbook, signed a check and handed it to Alberto. Alberto, all in tears, took the piece of paper and began to examine it.

"Is that a joke, Monsieur?"

"No, Alberto, this is not a joke, my name stands there, and they will accept this check in any bank of the world and cash it out or put it on your account without a question."

"A million Euros?"

"Yes. This is just paper. Pray and wait for your time. You and Augustine will live long life in joy. Only never forget God. Do you understand?"

Alberto stood on his knees all in tears and read *Nostro padre* in his Italian. Then he jumped up, and grabbed Cain's bag and suitcase.

"Monsieur, I am very grateful to you, may God help you and may God always be with you."

"Thanks, Alberto, now take the bag and the suitcase down and place them near the reception desk. Don't wait for me. You and I will not see each other again, so goodbye, Alberto. May God be with you. Yes, and it is also very important; remember, do not tell anyone, about our meeting. Don't tell anyone how you cured cancer. If you tell someone, I will come and send you to hell. You understood me?"

"Yes, Monsieur, I will not tell anyone."

Alberto was gone. Cain sat on the sofa and felt empty inside. This is when you live with constant pain every day, you get used to it, and then emptiness settles in your soul. He was soothed with seconds of joy when he helped desperate people who pray to God. Cain heard their every prayer and he understood that by helping them go their way, he became an instrument of the Lord God. It brought him joy for seconds, and then he returned back to a sad state. He was very tired of the planet Earth and everything connected with it. Cain knew the structure of any process on Earth, he knew the state of any matter, and he could penetrate into any animate being. Cain had been developing this gift over thousands of years. Archibald taught him a lot, to read minds and move around in space. But Cain was not interested in all this anymore, and he rarely used his gift. Once, when Cain was in church, he overheard a conversation of two women, they talked about the end of the world and about the Last Day that was described in the Bible. Cain caught himself on a thought how help to accelerate the arrival of the apocalypse, imperceptibly push the world into the abyss. Make it so, that THEY do not get angry. The telephone sounded sharply in the room and tore Cain from his reflections. He jumped up, abruptly went to the table and picked up the phone.

"Go ahead."

"Mr. Cai, are you all right? Aren't you late?"

"I'm on my way."

Cai put the phone down and headed for the exit. Jack stood in the hall. He stood upright like a telegraph pole and looked straight at his master.

"We will not make it in time."

"Well, then we'll take a private charter. I'm not a dog. I can be late, I can not arrive at all, they will have to take it anyway. We are still going to be here with you for a long time, we have nowhere to hurry."

"Fine. Will we have some tea?"

"Jack, start the engine, we're going, I don't like your jokes. Is the baggage in the car?"

"Yes, Boss. All is ready."

'Well, let's go."

Rolls Royce is of course a car for rich people. This is a very comfortable and very fast vehicle. So Cai bought this car for a good reason. He knew that he was buying quality, comfort and a ticket to higher societies. Because when a man arrives on such a car, the majority of the population of the planet Earth would try to take his pants off and perform a long and deep kiss in his ass. Moreover, this car helped save him time instead of long stories about the possibilities.

Cain also had a private plane and a helicopter, but he liked to watch people, so he often used public transport. In order to make people memorize him, Cai made himself business cards from pure gold. He knew that such a business card would not be thrown into the trash or get lost. In addition, before they are melted down, they will definitely call you at least one last time. When Cain arrived at the airport, the airport security chief met him. He ushered Cain and Jack to the ramp. The chief reminded him about the visa. Cain completely forgot that Jack needed a visa to Russia. Cain had a diplomatic passport and a Maltese passport; he could move freely anywhere in the world without unnecessary bureaucracy. Cain was escorted to the first class. Cain took out his phone and found his old friend in the list, who served in the Ministry of Communications. It was a special department at the Ministry of Defense, which was engaged in censorship and communication development. The guy's name was Vassily, Vasya. Vasya beside Russian, was fluent in German, English and Spanish. Vasya seemed to be a simple man. Vasya had a connection to any communications; he was engaged in the interception of cellular communications and any Internet provider. Although Vassily was an ordinary communication Colonel, he had in submission the best programmers in Russia. So this Vasya was not *just Vasya*.

"Hello, Vassily, how are you?"

"Hi, I haven't heard from you for a long time. When can we meet?"

"I am already departing to Moscow, flight 2393 Aeroflot."

"Wow, well done. I'll meet you."

"A guy flies with me; he doesn't have a visa, make him some certificate or something so that he has no problems."

"What's the guy's name?"

"Jack Mack."

"Sure, no problem."

"We take off, see you soon."

"Bye, bro!"

The plane took off, and Cain got lost in thought. He looked at the passengers and smiled.

'They all looked so important; they felt themselves the elected. First, they fly from Zurich to Moscow, and secondly, they fly first class. They all had significant faces. Yes, such pompous people control us and decide our fate. But soon, we will create a virus, and all these people will die a painful and inglorious death, somewhere in the hospital, where they do not accept credit cards and where everyone receives equally bad attitude. It remained for them to live very little, maybe a year, or maximum two. They will get into the world where there is no money and where everyone will receive his justice that he deserves. Cain knew that the virus would kill everyone who flew with him on the plane. He smiled wickedly. For him, these trifle people were of no value and no interest, they amused him. Still, there are very few smart people and they should remain alive. Once God flooded the whole Earth and left Noah. Now we will repeat this, but we will not destroy anything.'

Cain knew that he was preparing the end of the world. Hope did not leave him. He dreamed of meeting God every day.

"Will we drink, Boss?"

"Take whiskey. You know, I'm never drunk. For me, whiskey, like water for you, but you shouldn't drink too much."

Jack got up and waved his hand, the flight attendant came up to him.

"May we have some whiskey, please."

"I will serve it right now."

The girl rolled up her bar with drinks on wheels. With a smile on her face she asked, "What sort of whiskey do you prefer?"

"Any sort, please, two full glasses, two lemonades and two coffees, please."

The drinks filled the table. Cain looked at this performance with tired eyes, he knew that Jack was an alcoholic, he was shell-shocked, and had a sick head. He could not drink much, because when drunk he always thrust himself at people.

"Boss, let's drink to a soft landing."

Jack handed Cain a glass.

"Okay, let's drink. Only without your tricks, Jack."

They drank a glass of whiskey each, and washed it down with lemonade. Cain felt a bitter taste and thought how one can voluntarily drink such filth and even pay money for it.

"Listen Jack, I'll sleep a little."

"Boss, you are not sleeping. Are you tired of me?"

"No, Jack, I just have to think, we have a lot to do."

Cain took the first class tickets, because there were comfortable sleeping armchairs in the first class. He could lounge comfortably in the armchair and resign himself to meditation.

'The first stage is to find this Seraphim. I do not even know how to convince him to work with us, he is the Chosen One and ordinary human levers do not act on him. In addition, those selected ones have no weaknesses. God has endowed him with intelligence, intuition, and unlimited will power. This is a very difficult task. We did not have to persuade Noah. Noah didn't know that not all of the Earth was flooded with water. And this one, we do not know who he is. He is the new kind.'

Cai imagined how the plane was flying, he knew that outside the aircraft was minus fifty, the turbines revolve and create an air stream that keeps this iron bird in the air.

'If it were not for Archibald, who got tired of riding horses, then people would still move on the surface of the ground only, with a maximum speed of a running horse. Archibald wanted to move loads and people quickly, so he taught people to invent airships. God did not intervene in this process. People do not even think about how such a machine, weighing tens of tons of metal, rises into the air and flies at an extreme height and at an extreme speed. The plane does not flap its wings, but flies better, than any bird. Archibald appeared and created the design. Moreover, no one understands that this is the work of the Devil, as well as the mirror or as TV, Internet or a cell phone. Archibald created all these innovations to make his work easier for him. People are easy to manage. The person who knows the truth, protects himself from these traps. But nobody believes in God today. On the TV, there are clever men who can explain everything except the fact of human death or sudden death. On the TV, they show a permanent advertisement of debauchery and a blasphemous lifestyle. Archibald does not need to communicate with everyone; the TV and the Internet do this. All artists who advertise drinks, cigarettes, murder, violence and hectic lifestyle make fabulous money and thus attract all the other stupid people. Archibald is a genius; he invented the wheel and the eternal engine of human stupidity and sinfulness. Now it is time to put an end to this. It is high time to clean the Earth from filth, give it a break from the parasites.'

Flight time slipped quickly. The signal to fasten the seat belts buzzed, the plane descended to the landing. Cain turned off his perception of people. How many people Cai saved, how many people he helped, it was difficult to count. Cain did boundless good in the hope that God would forgive him and take him to THEMSELVES. Cain repented a thousand times, but this did would not work, and he tried not to interfere in human fates. Archibald decided to destroy humanity and Cain did not delve into it. So it pleased God. Jack was in a great mood; he flirted with flight attendants and constantly poured beer in himself. The plane landed smoothly, everything went like clockwork. The ramp drove over, the door opened and Vassily stood down at the airstairs, with a smile on his face and with open arms.

"Hello, my dear Cai, I wanted to see you for a long time, but even with my possibilities I cannot catch you, you do not leave a trace."

"Hello Vassily, I'm glad to see you too. Meet Jack. Jack is a proven man, so you can positively trust him."

Vassily got behind the wheel of a *Lexus*. They all got into his car. The vehicle headed to the exit, the staff of the frontier guard stood at the guard desk. Vassily stopped the car and rolled down the window; they recognized him.

"Wish health, Vassily Ivanovich, who are your passengers?"

"These are a Swiss diplomat and an American attaché coming with me. The documents are in order; we are going to the Ministry."

"*Bon Voyage.*"

The barrier raised, and the car smoothly drove onto the highway. Vassily continued the conversation.

"Listen, Cai, there are the documents for your friend Jack Mack in the glove compartment. I made him the council of justice, the certificate is valid, and introduced into all bases. There is a special mark for the police on the certificate so as not to answer too many questions. Now tell me, what else I can do for you."

"Dear Vasya, I need to find some monk, this is the first request, the second request, make me a clergyman, so to speak, officially, and find me two '*our*' novices of the church who are aware of this church theme. These novices should be very literate, perhaps after the theological academy. In addition, I need the priest's robe and all the necessary trifles, preferably used ones, so that it can be evident, that I have been wearing these clothes for years."

"What are you up to, Cain? Will you make a coup in the church?"

"No, I'm interested in your not devilish affairs. I need one specific person, this monk, I have to take him with me, and fly him to Germany."

"Why this masquerade? Let's just tie him up and put him on a plane. It will save us time and our strength."

"Strength is impossible to apply. It is necessary that he voluntarily boards the plane and flies with us."

"And what if he does not want? What then?"

"Then I will call out the wrath of God and thrust all our strength upon him."

"What is that supposed to mean? What does the wrath of God mean?"

"The wrath of God is to break all ten God's commandments in an attitude to this man. And I will break all the Laws, if a certain monk does not want to co-operate with us. All sin falls on me, but a shadow falls on him, this is enough for me to keep him away from God, because he will cause many troubles and people will curse him. A great many of people will curse him and he will feel very crowded and stuffy."

"Only God knows what's in your head, I wouldn't want to become your enemy. You can destroy anyone; grind into the dust! No one of those whom I know has such power and authority."

"I cannot destroy anyone or grind into the dust. It can do only God himself. We can only bring a person under attack. And the fate of man is decided only by God."

"Well, I saw it with my own eyes, how many people you killed. Was that so, how God decided?"

"Obviously, if I have a gun in my hand, aimed at you, and the gun is serviceable, live ammunition with fresh powder in the gun and nothing jams, and I consciously send a signal to my hand that puts the gun against your head and my finger executes the order and pulls the trigger, and the bullet, taking off from the muzzle, goes exactly through your head or your heart, which leads to instant death, then this is undoubtedly the Will of the Lord God. Otherwise, this would be different. However, if a person is under the protection of the Lord God and you want to kill him, then this will never happen. Never. If you do not believe me, then I can give you the opportunity to kill Seraphim. But, knowing initially the outcome of this case, I will dissuade you, because I know what will happen to you further, and to anyone, who has crappy intentions against Seraphim. Everyone will die various painful deaths. Someone from diarrhea and someone would be just stupidly ridden over by a truck. And that would happen much earlier before they begin to act. That is why he cannot be just shoved into the plane by strength; he must want it himself, otherwise all will end painfully. For everyone except me. He probably already knows that we are looking for him. And he knows that we have no bad intentions and everything is voluntary. So, we come in peace to him. Where are we heading?"

"I will settle you in the *National*, firstly because this is the center, and secondly, this is the safest place in Russia."

"I know; Lenin lived there with Krupskaya. This hotel had always been interesting, interesting in the political sense. Now, of course, this hotel has lost its meaning, but its location is very interesting for every foreigner. I assume, today there still is full overlistening and video surveillance of all the guests in the hotel?"

"No, this is impossible! Here I guarantee you complete privacy! How could you think so?"

"Then bring me a jammer."

"Fine."

The *National Hotel* is located in the very center of Moscow, near the Kremlin and Red Square. It was built in 1903. Different officials, princes and revolutionaries lived there at different times. Lenin himself, a friend of Archibald, sacrificed millions of people. He himself did not even understand how much good he did. He banned faith in God, destroyed and forbade the church. With his help, THEY quickly saw those souls who truly believed and at the cost of their lives defended the faith in God. They were executed, but they found peace forever. The *National Hotel* is a live hotel, where the souls of atheists, scoundrels, and revolutionaries who were eager to kill people, live. All these souls are attached to the walls of the hotel. And Cain saw them all, they could fulfill any of his wishes, in return for a minute attention. Cain knew much more than he said aloud. Vassily knew that Cain was an unusual person, so he treated him with great respect and was a little afraid of him. He remembered that when Cain was in Afghanistan, he got under a deadly shelling. The clothes on Cain were completely burned; he got up barefoot with a black face and began to collect metal balls. Nobody knew what kind of balls they were and why he needed them. And when he entered the tent, he asked the soldiers to give him new clothes and a glass of water to wash himself. Cain saw that Vassily had his legs crippled. Vassily lay shell-shocked on the ground, he stared at one point with a glass look. Cain found a metal flask of water and whispered a few words on the water that changed its structure. He splashed the water on Vassily's face, and he came to his senses. He woke up and realized everything at once. Cain told him that he should drink all the water from the flask and this would strengthen the immune system and his body will restore itself. Vassily drank everything to the last drop. That was how they met and became lifelong friends. After this water, Vassily never got sick, and looked young for his age. Therefore, Vassily felt boundless devotion to Cain. He appreciated that Cain saved him, he remembered that, and never forgot. Vassily wanted to prove once again that he was grateful to Cain, so he organized the best suite for him. Cain realized that the Russians had no idea of what service was. The Russians do not feel the duty to serve. They can fool around, but not long enough. Russian do not know how to constantly, for a long time, to do something well and efficiently. Soon they get tired and start doing shit. And the problem was that there were not enough pure-blooded Russians, because the Tatar yoke has mixed their blood for many centuries. Though the Russians think they are Russians, their blood is Tatar, nomadic. They cannot live in one place, and make quality products or provide good service; all they need is a fight and scuffle. In this, they are excellent. Therefore, in the *National* there is a service, but it seems to be compulsory. The same goes for the interior and the cuisine. The only good thing was the price. Although Cain did not pay, he knew the prices of this hotel. For this money, they could try a little harder. Cain did not want to upset Vassily and agreed to check in this hotel.

"Vasya, I'll go for a walk, and you check me in. Good?"

"No problem, I'll be waiting for you in the room. We can go eat something; they cooked delicious food here."

"I know the food is delicious. I will walk a little, and then we will think a bit later."

Cai got out of the car and went to the crossing in the direction of the Kremlin. Vassily got out of the car and signaled the receptionist from the hotel. The doorman approached him and called a porter by radio. Bags were loaded and dragged into the hotel; the car was parked in the underground parking. Vassily, together with the American, went to the hotel, and approached the manager at the reception desk. Vassily was recognized and immediately issued the keys. They did not check them, because the general director regularly used the services and aid of Vassily. And this time they did not ask questions and did not take the money. They simply gave them the largest, most spacious and multi-bed room, where once probably lived the masters of life.

"Thanks. Which floor?"

"The third floor."

They ascended silently to the third floor and entered the most spacious hotel suite. The place was very pompous; antique furniture, sculptures, statues, carpets, tapestries, paintings were everywhere. This was definitely a museum of the last millennium, not a hotel for the relaxation and fun. Bronze rams and medieval characters carefully watched every your step. In this room, you cannot poke in the nose or scratch your ass. Everybody was carefully watched, and the walls listened to the least rustle. Jack also realized that he could not relax here with call-girls and coke, as he did at home. This was not a rest, it would be round-the-clock work pretending to be a decent American citizen. He wanted to booze, booze heavily, pour liquor and eat cocaine with his ass, and then embrace many different beauties, many beautiful bodies. Jack felt squeezed in his chest; it was a nostalgia for the debauchery. He understood that he needed to control himself.

"Here in these walls the revolutionaries were planning coup d'états and terrorist attacks."

"Here you feel as in a museum, why did you choose such an inconvenient hotel for us? I'm afraid to sleep here, I will sleep standing and dressed. Here I have the impression like at a cemetery where the dead are watching you. This hotel can be advised only to enemies; one doesn't propose that to friends."

"I didn't do for you. I did it for Cai. For him, this is the best hotel. He will communicate with his friends and it would be easier for him to come up with a plan of action here. And such a move requires peace and tranquility. But if you arrange a brothel here, then it would be impossible for him to think and act rationally. I'll leave now and prepare the priest's clothes, I received information that some priest died two days ago. I will go and take away his things; they should be tried on and hemmed if necessary."

"Okay, I'll go to bed. This is the gloomiest hotel in my whole life. I will try to get a nap for an hour."

"See you."

Cain was already standing on the Red Square, in the heart of Moscow, near the Kremlin and the Mausoleum. He wanted to talk to Lenin. Cain knew Lenin since his early childhood. That red-haired curly toddler faced a great trial, and strangely enough, God permitted all his actions and later severely punished everyone including him. He died in agony from the luetic decomposition of the brain. Namely, the body dies, and the soul is tied to the body and in full consciousness lives with the body, which slowly and inevitably decomposes. This is the worst punishment, to see worms crawling on you. God gives different punishments, so it is better to quietly live this life and then happily and eagerly go to God than ride around standing proudly on an armored car, and then lie prone and motionless for several hundred years in an open coffin and watch worms unhurriedly eating your body. The slower you go, the farther you will get. *Festina lente*. Hurry slowly.

Who was Lenin? He was a German Jew, Johan Kochenschwatz, whose mother was a Russian-speaking Jewish woman; his father was a German Jew. Little Johan has been talking to his mother in Russian since childhood. At a young age, he drew well and played the violin, he was an ordinary *wunderkind* from a good Jewish family. He knew little about Russia, later he would be taught to rule it and made a legend for the Russian people. Since the very beginning of the Russian Empire, in 1713, it was established, that the Russian people should have either a German or a Jew as a manager, still better a German Jew.

The Orthodox Christianity is accepted as the official religion of the Russian Empire. Christianity is a religion for servants and slaves, it teaches to obey, and not to rack your brain. Jews invented Christianity in order to control the slaves, for whom alcohol is permitted and adultery is not punished, a Christian must forgive everyone, and cannot take revenge. Slaves must be submissive. Judaism does not teach to be docile, and Jews are not threatened by the Devil in the synagogue. That is why the Jews, after Archibald and God, rule the entire planet. Cain met Johan when he went to a music school. Cain asked little Kochenschwatz, Lenin-to-be, what he wanted to become, and little Johan said that he wanted to become the Chancellor of Germany. Archibald had a better and more fascinating plan for Johan. Archibald, as always, acts globally. When Johan turned 19 years old, he signed an agreement with Archibald and signed it with his blood. Johan had a simple desire, he dreamed of becoming famous, so that he would be honored and remembered for another hundred years after his death. Archibald fulfilled the request, but as always a little modified it, therefore everyone remembered Lenin, Volodya Ulyanov, a man who did not exist, and no one knew Johan Kochenschwatz, he had to forget about his relatives, his family and friends. He was taken to Switzerland, where he began his training for the sabotage work in Russia. For all Johan Kochenschwatz has died. When you make a contract with the Devil, you need to know that everything will be the other way around. Lenin lay in his tomb in his Mausoleum. Cain was not allowed to enter there.

Cain did not elaborate and mesmerize or bribe the guards. Lenin was not that interesting to him. He just wanted to have fun again.

Cain walked around and saw how Moscow was embellished. Everywhere there were beautiful cafes and shops, people from the whole world walked around the square. It was evident that this was a big metropolis where big money rotates. Muscovites did not spare money for luxury; almost all cars were top-class. Any civilization is self-destructive, and destroys itself independently, be it Russia or America or Japan. The speed of life is growing and people permanently lack time. Civilization is convenient, but you have to pay for everything. Cain walked along the Red Square and along the streets, went into the GUM, bought himself a *Komandirskie* watch with a red star, the symbol of Lucifer, and a compass, and decided to return to the hotel.

He must find Seraphim. Cain recognized that this was his last mission. He headed for the hotel in quick pace. He walked to the door of the hotel and the door attendant greeted him and opened the door, Cain nodded his head in return and thrust twenty dollars into his hand. Cain knew his room and immediately began climbing the stairs to the third floor. The door of his room was closed; Cain kicked the door and shouted loudly in English, "Jack, mazzafaka, open up!"

"You got it, Boss!"

Jack was already half-drunk; a large golden cross dangled from his neck.

"Jack, where did you get this cross?"

"Vassily has just brought the clothes."

"Put down everything back. This is all for me, and this is not a masquerade."

Jack looked at Cain earnestly, took off the cross and put it on the table. Cain took the golden cross in his hands and understood that this accessory will not work. Gold is the metal of Lucifer, this metal is forbidden to believers. Strictly prohibited. The wooden or silver cross was in demand. Vassily appeared in the hallway and happily said, "Here, look, I got everything."

"In these garments you can only go to a nightclub, everything is made of gold and precious stones. This is blasphemy; a true servant of the Lord will never allow himself to sully the symbol of faith in God with the metal of the Devil. These stupid people want to rise above others and thus assign themselves the phony importance. I need a modest and worn monk's robe and a wooden cross; give this junk back, I cannot wear it."

"Well, it's a piece of cake, now I'll run and fetch it; I know a priest here, he will give it to me. It won't costs anything."

"Choose my size right away, the cassock should be old, worn, the cross should also be old on a leather cord."

"Okay, Cai, give me half an hour."

"I am not in a hurry. Without a real priest's cassock, we just keep shifting from one foot to the other. So do your best and also find me at least one novice, nimble, not stupid."

"You got it."

Cain fell into a large leather armchair and turned on the TV. He watched mostly news, incidents in the world. The news showed strikes in Greece, in Athens. He put away the remote control and, with a smile on his face, watched cars burn in the streets of the Greek capital. He paid no attention to Jack, who was feeling blue and could not get what was going on. Jack poured himself a whiskey. The whiskey was called *Kraken*, Cain found it in the Duty-Free. When he saw this bottle and its label, he immediately bought several bottles at once. He liked the word *Kraken*, and the whiskey was soft and pleasant. Cain looked at Jack and said, "Do not languish, get dressed and go somewhere to the club. I can manage without you. Do you have money?"

"I have 500 bucks."

"For Moscow, this is nothing; take a couple of thousands from my suitcase and get the hell out of here. I'll call you when I need you. Do not turn off the phone. You have time until tomorrow, for tomorrow we will fly away to another city."

"Thank you, Boss. I go."

"Have a nice time."

The door slammed and Cain immersed into himself. He saw how this world and people deteriorated. Immorality swallowed all, people turned away from God. Homosexuality, pedophilia, sodomy have become commonplace.

'We must cure this world. Make it promptly and without delay.'

Cain wanted to see self-confident rich people who think they rule this world die in torments. He wanted to see how a vile African tribe king who had betrayed his own kin would rot alive and the flies settle in his head.

'A lot of betrayal is around us, honesty and decency have become ridiculous. Did not God, did not Allah in the Qur'an say that the end of time would come when decency becomes ridiculous and honest people become outcasts of society? Now this time has come. I will take Jack and Vasya with me, the others will die painfully, and their souls will burn on fire, Archibald said so. For a thousand years, they will be cleared and then they will be given another chance, they will be returned to the Earth.'

Cain wanted to develop a virus that will kill slowly, in twenty-one days. He has already seen how they are all fussing, running around the doctors, the doctors shrug, the doctors themselves become infected, then they go to the healers, and then, before they die, they crawl into the church to pray to God. Unfortunately, this is the only way out and the only solution. Cain wanted people to have time to think about their own life and all wrongdoings. Cain mentally returned to his childhood, when there were no people, he remembered how spacious the world was and it breathed quite differently. Cain knew that everything would be the same again. The Earth will be cleared of filth, of dirt, of factories, of rockets, of stupid people. Very little time is left. If Seraphim fails, then he will look for another way out to kill everyone. The Lord God will give the worthy new bodies and everything they need. Cain listened, and heard the noise of cars that kept on moving, he heard thousands thoughts of people who were rushing to and fro along the streets, who were driving their cars.

"Not a single decent thought, same old shit only."

Cain said this aloud, though there was no one in the room. Suddenly Cain smelled vanilla and cinnamon and thought, 'You flew here again. What the fuck do you want?'

Cain heard the answer in his head, 'Halt Cain, do not do something that you will regret for a long time!'

"Kiss my ass with your good for nothing advice. Take me away and you won't need to ask me for anything."

'The time has not come yet, you have very little left to wait, be patient a little more and THEY will forgive you!'

"How long should I wait? Another thousand years to look at this shit, those stupid animals, and live in this shit? If that's the way it is, then I'll clean the world. I will arrange beauty, purity, and then I will wait another thousand years alone. I hate humans. Instead of whispering to me here, ask THEM, let THEY take me to THEMSELVES. I have repented a million times and served THEM for thousands years together with Archibald. And the matter is not too tricky, people are stupid, it costs me only to pull out a piece of gold, as they immediately do everything that I want in spite of all the commandments of the Lord God. Nothing new happens, every time the same case. First, I offer them money, then power, and then they break all the Commandments and thus every time and again. I am tired. They deserve to be killed all, I will send them a plague, so as not to waste time. May THEY return them to the times of the Inquisition, and let their heads be chopped off every day, they deserve it. You read thoughts, you agree with me. These people are not worthy a chance."

'What is more important? Those small people or your fate? THEY told you not to interfere and wait for your time. Will you go against the Will of the Lord God? You know what will happen next?'

"What could be worse? Worse than now?"

'You will be turned into a common man, you will be thrown back to the beginning of times, and you will be born and die until one cycle ends. And one cycle is 10,000 years. This is very wicked and painful. And even if you are recognized as a holy and most worthy person during your human life, even then your term will not change, your memory will be removed, and remade again. You do not feel time now that you are immortal, but if you are turned into a mortal man, without memory, you will derive your subsistence from a garbage can and thank God for everything. You know that we are not bluffing.'

Cain frowned. He had a lump in his throat, his temples boomed, and the feeling was as if his head was going to burn and explode. Cain opened the window and jumped out into the street, head first.

Cain lay motionless on the sidewalk; a large pool of blood was expanding. The onlookers stopped at a loss, not knowing how to help him. Some man came up and put two fingers on Cain's neck.

"Alive, he is alive! I feel his pulse. Do not touch him; his spinal cord may be damaged."

Cain fell into darkness. He felt warm, as if plunged into a hot bath. Then he heard his mother's lullaby. And then he felt himself a baby, they took him in their arms and held against their chest, this was his elder brother Abel. Abel pulled him closer and talked to him, "This was You, my Brother who was chosen by God, not me, it is You who are THEIR Hand on the Earth. I was not worthy of a chance, I sacrificed animals. So God laid his hopes on you. Do not let THEM down. Stop yourself."

Cain wanted to answer, but the words stuck in his throat, and only a thin squeak escaped.

Then Archibald stepped forward.

"Now, where did you get with your follies? Are you in a doubt? Wake up Cain, we are waiting for you."

Meanwhile, people began to gather near the body on the asphalt. The door attendant from the hotel ran up and immediately saw his generous guest of the hotel. He instantaneously pulled out a cell phone and dialed Vassily. Everyone in the hotel knew Vassily, and respected him more than the director.

"Hello Vassily, this is Arthur, the doorman from the hotel. Our foreign guest jumped out of the window and crashed his head. I called an ambulance. They say he seems alive."

"What foreigner? Is this that sturdy American?"

"No, this is the other, the solid one, that Englishman or Swiss."

"Stay with him and do not leave him, if the ambulance arrives, sit down with them, we will be in touch. Report to me everything that happens. This man is important to me as a father; he saved my life. We are obliged to save him and bring back to life!"

"I understand. I will be in touch."

Instantly, an ambulance arrived and the medics jumped out of the car. They pulled a stretcher out of the wagon and instantly laid it nearby. Arthur the doorman ran up to one of the doctors and asked who was in charge. He was lucky; the chief of the ambulance brigade was standing before him.

"This person is our foreign honored guest, I ask you to talk with our management."

Arthur quickly dialed Vassily.

"Comrade Vassily, the doctors have arrived; I'll put them on the phone."

"Go ahead!"

The doctor took the phone from Arthur's hand and put it to his ear.

"Hello, listen to me attentively! My name is Vassily Titov; I am a colonel of counterintelligence. This foreign citizen, who fell out of the window, is our very important witness. Accordingly, I ask you to treat him carefully and do everything necessary to save him. All the expenses I take on myself, I am in a hurry to see you right now. Please, let me know which hospital you are taking him to."

"To the nearest hospital, where it is possible to artificially support a person's life. The address is 2, Romanov Lane. First, we need to know what damage your foreign guest had suffered."

Behind his back, the doctor heard a shout and applause. He could not understand what was happening. He quickly began to push through the crowd. People screamed, whistled and applauded. The doctor could not believe his eyes, the foreigner was standing upright on his feet near the stretcher, all smeared in blood. Arthur the doorman ran up to him and grabbed his arm.

"What the hell is this? Well, urgently put the patient on a stretcher!"

The foreigner spoke in English, "Thanks. It's okay! I am fine!"

He pulled a handful of crumpled dollar bills out of his pocket and shoved them to the doctor.

"I am fine! I'm going to the hotel."

Arthur was holding him under his arm. Blood pulsed from Cain's head. He turned to Arthur and spoke loudly in English, intensely suggesting everyone by the power of thought, "Everything is okay with me, we are going to the hotel, tell them to go, and thank them. I gave them some money."

Arthur and Cain headed to the hotel. Doctors and pedestrians stood astonished. They did not turn around and entered the hall of the hotel, followed by the doctor from the ambulance.

"Let me at least treat your wounds."

"Let us do that in the room, third floor."

They took the elevator upstairs. Along the hallway, Cain was already walking on his feet. The door was open; Cain walked in and sat down on the sofa, his head thrown back. The doctor walked around him and began to examine his head. The skin got off the head, it was necessary to sew. Suddenly Cain said in a strange dry Russian, "No need to sew. Clean the wound, bandage it, and that's all."

Cain knew many languages, among them Russian, but nearly always he spoke English or German. The doctor was shocked. He pulled the necessary instruments out of his surgeon's chest and began to treat the wounds on Cain's head. The doctor could not get rid of thinking about falling from such a height; he could not understand how this foreigner survived.

"I stayed alive because God wanted it. Do you understand me?"

"Yes. And do you remember how you fell?"

"I remember my Brobel Abel, my Mother Eve, I remember Lucifer, I remember the conversation with Archangel Michael. I remember rage and that is all. God told me to live, so I mentioned enough facts. Or this is not enough for you?"

The doctor accurately washed all the wounds and folded the skin back.

"It is necessary to sew, the wounds will heal for a long time."

"Wash and bandage. And thanks. Goodbye."

"As you wish."

The doctor carefully bandaged Cain's head. Cain called Arthur by force of thought and ordered him to bring the suitcase from another room. Arthur brought the suitcase and handed it to Cain. Cain took a wad of cash and held it out to the doctor. The doctor definitely refused to take the money.

Vassily burst into the room, he was all sweaty and his eyes were burning.

"Cai, what was it?"

"Everything is fine, Vasya, relax."

"Tell me what's wrong with him?"

"He has multiple injuries; it is advisable at first to sew the skin on his head. But he decidedly and repeatedly refused. I cannot force him."

"Clear. Do not tell anyone about this incident. Good?"

"Yes. I understand."

The doctor left the hotel room and headed for the exit. Vassily poured himself a full glass of rum and drank it in one gulp, then sat down in silence, and took his head in his hands. It was evident that he had warried a lot in that short time.

"Everything's fine, Vasya, don't you worry. Have you forgotten that I am immortal?"

"Aha. After jumping down from the third floor window, right on your head, even the immortal remain without a head."

Cain looked odd with his head bandaged; his face was gloomy, his eyes were sad. Vassily immediately noticed this change.

"Cai, Bro, what happened? Who threw you out the window?"

"I jumped out myself. I was fucked up by those whisperers in my head."

"What will we do next? You need to sew up your head."

"It will heal itself; tomorrow I will be as good as new. The skin is primitive; it does not need a lot of time to recover. I have a capsule with a special solution in Zurich, it heals skin and tissue in one hour. Without my capsule and without this solution there will be no trace in 7 days. Tomorrow only the scars will remain, but all the wounds will heal. Tell me, Brother Vassily, did you find the priest's clothes?"

"I didn't have time to find your size, the doorman called me and I immediately arrived. I've been to the laundry, we had everything washed and cleaned. I have found everything necessary."

"Well, get a car, let's go for a fitting. I have to get dressed today, and today we must find this Seraphim. Vassily, did you find Seraphim?"

"Yes, three months ago he was in New Athos, this is in Abkhazia. There I will ask around the place; I could not find out anything else."

"Well, that is enough; tomorrow we fly to Abkhazia."

"There is no airport there in Abkhazia, so we are flying to Sochi and from there go by car."

They left the hotel, got into the car, and headed for the monastery. Vassily immediately phoned to the hegumen and warned him about their arrival. It was a short drive, the Holy Father waited for them; without any further questions, the priest ushered them to the laundry. Cain was appropriately clothed and felt himself an ordinary monk. The inured bandaged head and scratched face, black as charcoal burning eyes, appealed to a mendicant friar. Cain looked persuasive. Everybody silently admired him because visually he perfectly resembled a hermit, the only minus was the lack of a beard and a neat appearance, very clean and well-groomed hands. But all this was fixable.

Profession is a state of the soul. Cain felt himself a monk, he knew the Bible by heart, so he could take around anyone, even a professional theologist. He decided to recall himself the Russian language, namely the Old Church Slavonic language. Cain had learned long ago that any knowledge came in the process; he knew that he would recall everything necessary. Cain did not have to learn languages; he memorized any information from the first time, because thus God had created him. He remembered perfectly the Old Babylonian language, the outcome of all next languages. It was a highly sophisticated language; the words had mighty power, but then everything changed, when God gave each tribe a different tongue so that they would not talk between each other and plot a conspiracy against THEM. The older generation still could understand each other, but their children already spoke in primitive tribal talks. God decided to reduce the power of the brain of each individual. How did it happen? God changed the composition of oxygen so that the brain could not develop even a half of its power. Our brain works at 5% capacity, that is its maximum; when we start developing our brain, we are getting smarter in one sphere, but we are getting dumber in other branches. God took away our minds, because people did not know how to use them.

The inhabitants of Babylon were very mentally developed, they did not need doctors, there were no scientists, and they lived as one organism. They renounced the Creator, they created the descendants themselves, they did not give birth to children by the natural way, they grew offspring artificially in test tubes with the modified DNA, they did not grow older and almost did not die. They calculated any probable risk, there were no diseases at all, and they did not fight in wars. Everything was perfect, but they became distant from God, so God decided to make people mortal and more humble, so that every man stood for himself only, experienced hatred, envy, and fought in wars. God had sent the humanity back to the primitive state.

And as the scoundrel Darwin stated, that people were descended from monkeys, then in chronological order, God turned mentally developed people into apes. Well, except for Darwin himself, Darwin was the only one descendant from a monkey.

Cain knew that development of humanity goes in a spiral, the humankind develops, and then returns back to the Stone Age. As soon as the peoples forget God, God clears the counter and starts everything anew from the very beginning. The human soul travels in time, so if a person becomes lavish, emaciated and considers himself a god, the Lord God sends this soul back to the Stone Age, where this poor soul lives in a smoky cave and eats grass and worms from the mud. Only through pain and suffering, a person turns to God again, and begins to believe sincerely.

The rain of fire, or the worldwide flood, or the deadly virus, everything comes back again in its turn, because people are trashy and ungrateful. Sometimes it is necessary to shake them up; suffering and pain purify the human soul. Now, Cain did not comprehend, why THEY were trying to stop him. Why? Wasn't it the best time now to end this debauchery? Cain knew that he would create a virus that would read human DNA one way or another. But if THEY would not want Cain to launch this virus, then this never happens. Cain knew that God rules the worlds and decides the outcome of any affair. Therefore, Cain was sure that he could launch the virus only with the highest permission of the Lord God.

In addition to his garments, Cain obtained an old, shabby leather-bound Bible with bookmarks and a roughly made hand polished wooden cross. Cain hanged the cross on his neck and opened the Bible. He wanted to recall the Old *Rusian* Church language and commenced to reading.

Cain began reading aloud, "Then I saw a great white throne and him who was seated on it. Earth and sky fled from his presence, and there was no place for them. And I saw the dead, great and small, standing before the throne, and books were opened. Another book was opened, which is the book of life. The dead were judged according to what they had done, as recorded in the books. The sea gave up the dead that were in it, and death and Hades gave up the dead that were in them; and each person was judged according to what he had done."

"Good for you!" Cain praised himself.

The phone rang, Cain picked up the gadget.

"Go ahead."

"Where are you, why can't I hear you? What the hell happened?"

"My dear Archibald, it's okay, I put on my priest's cassock and read the Bible in Old *Rusian*, and I am making progress."

"Why do you think you need to transform yourself to such an extent? Try not to overdo! I can't get in touch with you all day. What's going on in there?"

"It happened so, that the damn whisperers fucked up my brain and I got upset. Now I have put on well-prayed garments, and the cross of a monk who died in the cellar during a prayer. This cross has a long history and probably all these things in some way affect me. We will be in touch; tomorrow, or maybe today, I will fly to Abkhazia. I'll call you; don't worry, I'll accomplish the mission."

"Okay, and stop freaking out. They told me you jumped down from the third floor headfirst and now you are going around with your dudes with your head all bandaged. You do look ridiculous."

"Well, if I'm ridiculous, don't look at me. I know that you know everything. All goes according to the plan."

"Your spontaneous attempt of diving down into the concrete asphalt just because you were given a good advice did not come in my plans. Your notorious pride will ruin you. God had punished you for your pride, yet, you still do not know how to obey and submit. THEY wanted to teach you a lesson, but you didn't become a trifle wiser after all that very long time."

"Yes, I agree, I am far from being perfect. I know who I am. I know that I was the best of all the people that God has created. So, perhaps, regarding this, I was the Chosen One? I always obeyed God and never broke His Commandments until I got a good friend. A good friend who also loves to whisper in my ear. Do not you treat me. If you want to do something, do it. I have no fear. Fear does not exist."

"I'm not going to scare you, do whatever you choose. I just told you that after those thousands of years you still remain a narcissistic fool. Over."

Archibald threw down the phone and it shattered into fragments. He hated talking on the phone, he felt himself a monkey. He always talked to any person through his mind, bur here he had to pick up the phone, because he had lost Cain, and that was not clear and pleasant. During all these times, Archibald got used to Cain and therefore did not want to lose him. This was the first accident in all the time, he lost contact with his disciple and this was an ominous token, and certainly *not a coincidence*. The time has come. Archibald, with the help of his loyal servants Rothschilds, Rockefellers and Morgans, created hopeless poverty in the world with painted paper and empty promises. His servants, assholes, issue plain colored pieces of paper on the printing machine, and for those papers, people kill each other, which makes God very unhappy about the humankind, He is sorry, that His creatures are so stupid, and sell their precious souls for funny niggly wiggly. Those owners of the money-printing machine are completely subject to the Devil.

Archibald loves revolutions and wars. His first task is to destroy Islam. The Devil's servants created terrorist organizations, and then they bombed the entire Islamic world, ostensibly in the fight against terror. Islam for Archibald is a thorn in his flesh. He ordered his demons to bomb and destroy all Islamic countries, preferably bomb them to smithereens. Especially, he wants to burn down all the archives, museums, and books. Islam must be considered a dangerous religion so that people feared Islam. Let them better drink alcohol, blaspheme God, use drugs, eat pork and smoke tobacco; let them lead a repugnant lifestyle; let them drown in sodomy and debauchery. Archibald understands that the faster sodomy and blasphemy spread, the faster his mission on the Earth is accomplished. Archibald, who is named the Devil and Lucifer, hates people, he despises them. Therefore, Archibald helps to establish snack bars with junk food, as well as advertise factories, producing sweet harmful soda pop all around the world, so that people eat junk food, drink dead water, and move away from God. TV and the Internet are the influence on everyone, in addition to harmful food; all this contributes to the separation from God. Sodomy promotion is highly paid too. Gay parades, homosexuality, pedophilia spread at the speed of a raging fire in the dry forest. In every country, where the so-called "democratic" governments rule, homosexuality is accepted and propagated as something absolutely normal and harmless. They all hate the Commandments of the Lord God and mock the believers. Islam is a grave menace that thwarts Archibald.

Archibald thought aloud, "If God orders me, I, with great joy, will kill everyone, absolutely everyone. I will burn the whole planet in an instant. After that, THEY will take me back to THEMSELVES. THEY will find out that I was right, I repented, and I will worship absolutely any creature THEY give breath to, even if it is the most stupid and ungrateful beast, like a human being. I will kneel down and will stand so until THEY allow me to get up from my knees. I never will repeat this error again. If they could only make it quick..."

Archibald realized that Cain should be followed up. For this task, he should call the proper person. Archibald summoned the trusted man, whose soul had been shackled to his corpse for many years. That was his favorite, Johan Kohenschwatz.

Archibald thought about him, and he appeared instantly, "I obey you, My Lord, what can I do for you?"

"Follow up Cain and report to me everything, be with him constantly."

"I'll do everything you order. Permit me to commence?"

"Get down to work."

Archibald loved betrayers; everything was always simple and easy with them. In general, Archibald loved unprincipled people.

Meanwhile, in Moscow, Cain was in a hurry. He already collected all the belongings, and rushed to the airport. He wanted to buy plane tickets to Sochi personally. Cain paid no attention to the conversation in the car; he was silent all the way. He knew that he was on the edge of events and soon the world would change radically. He knew that his life on the planet Earth was nearing its end. Suddenly, Cain was distracted from his thoughts and sensed the presence of a lost soul. The atmosphere in the car became stuffy and unpleasant, as if somebody had spoilt the air. Everyone suspiciously looked at each other.

"Volodya, is that you?"

"Yes, dear Cai, the Boss put me on you."

Everyone in the car fell silent and looked slightly surprised at Cain.

Cain smiled and said, "My friends, meet Vladimir Ilyich Ulianov-Lenin himself, we are accompanied by the Leader of the world lumpen-proletariat. Our friend Archibald sent this lost soul after us, he would follow up and report on us. I understand him; this is by far better than lying motionless in a closed stuffy dusty sarcophagus in the Mausoleum."

"But, Cai, I don't see anyone!"

"Dear Vassily, you people, won't see anything. God gave you eyes, but you do not see anything; God gave you ears, but you do not hear anything; God gave you a heart, but you do not believe. I smell him by his odor; he stinks of old rags. There, his mausoleum is not ventilated, so he stinks of stuffy old things, like sweaty dirty socks."

"Boss, are you kidding?"

"Yes, Jack, I was joking. I see human souls, and I see angels, but you cannot see them. God limited everything to you. Limited and that was rightly done. Otherwise, Lenin would tell you how sorry he was that he sold his soul to the Devil. If people could communicate with vagabond souls, that would have changed everything. People would pray to God and would not long for either money or power, knowing the price. And the price is very high. People get for a couple of years power and money, paying in return with thousands years of slavery. Every person who had suffered, has a debt to be returned, and if a million people suffered because of one person, then he will pay back to everyone. This may last several thousand years, before he is given a chance to return to the human body and prove his loyalty to God. A soul like Volodya's will serve the Devil forever."

"How dreadful it sounds."

"Yes, dear friends, be aware! Living on the Earth, be careful and very careful with your actions and words. You will be responsible for everything. God will not talk to you, they will count you, weigh you and send you to where you deserve. You're all lucky to meet me. I advise you all to pray earnestly for the rest of your life and hope that THEY will forgive. We will now find out exactly where Seraphim dwells."

"How?"

"*Tovarishch* Lenin will lead us there."

"You know, dear Cain, I am forbidden to talk to you."

"I need the exact whereabouts of Seraphim."

"He went up to the mountains in Abkhazia. Lives in the forest."

"And more precisely?"

"It's about 18 kilometers From New Athos, near the river Aapsta, he washes himself there. A monk from the New Athos monastery can guide you there. Well, actually, I can help you too."

"Have you been to Abkhazia?"

"Yes."

"Well, and how it is to you?"

"This is a country where there is no religion, but God is present."

"You are a fool Volodya! God is present everywhere!"

"I know, but there it is different. You will see yourself."

They got out of the car, Vassily and Jack had already become friends, so Vassily decided to accompany them to Abkhazia. Without any problems, they approached the ticket desk of the Aeroflot and bought three tickets.

"Have you find a novice for me?"

"I have, Boss, but we can handle it without him."

"Do you know church rites and customs?"

"No, I don't know, but Seraphim anyway knows who we are, so why fool around?"

"This is true."

They sat in a cafe and waited for check-in time to the plane. Everyone was in a great mood. Cain knew that little was left, the last step. If God did not send this idea with a virus, everything would be the same as always. It was a challenge, he wanted to look into the eyes of dying people, he knew that everyone would die. *Bayer Lab* will create a virus that will kill them all.

Check-in time began, and Vassily called his comrade, who served at the airport. Ten minutes later, a jolly man approached them, embracing Vassily and whispering something in his ear. Vassily, too, was glad to see his old friend and colleague. They chatted and recalled old times. Vassily found Cain's eyes and by facial expression, mentally signaled to follow them. Jack carried the suitcases, and Cain in the monk's cassock walked with a relaxed gait. He felt great. Vladimir Ilyich obediently and invisibly followed them. They walked through the service corridors and fulfilled all the formalities. Nobody paid attention to them. They walked in immediately to the departure lounge. Landing on the flight was not yet announced. Vassily's friend pulled out a walkie-talkie and said something on the radio, while continuing to communicate lively with Vassily. Another man approached them, and Vassily briefly explained him the procedure of boarding the plane. When the door was opened for landing, their entire team was let in before the rest of the passengers. Cain did not care; he did not pay attention to the bustle. They went aboard the plane and settled in the first class. Jack was in a great mood and offered Vassily to take a drink. Vassily did not refuse. Jack had a large bottle of whiskey with a picture of the sea monster on the label. They asked for glasses and a pretty flight attendant immediately brought them glasses, cups and juice.

Vassily and Jack said cheers and immediately emptied their full glasses.

The day was very busy. Jack talked freely and began to recall stories from his childhood, and Vassily eagerly kept up the conversation. Vassily knew English very well. By the way, the spread of the English language is an attempt to create a new Babylonian language, a uniting language for all continents. This also brings us closer to the end of the world we know.

Vassily told how Cain saved his life and pulled him out of the shelling. He was already a little drunk; he was overgesticulating and showing his boundless gratitude to Cain. Jack was silent and recalled his acquaintance with Cain. Jack was a juvenile murderer, and if it were not for Cain, Jack would have been roasted on an electric chair. Cain taught him, sent him to the college, then to the army, and after serving in the army, Jack studied at the best university in Alabama, in the city of Tuscaloosa. Cain devoted to Jack a lot of strength and knowledge, and Jack understood that without Cain his life would go the other way, the wrong way, and would be hopelessly ruined. Therefore, Jack also felt boundless devotion and gratitude to Cain. When Jack was 13 years old, he turned on the gas in the house where he lived with his mother and his stepfather. The vile stepfather constantly bullied Jack, and his mother was unable to protect him. When his mother went to night shifts at the hospital, Jack had to stay at home alone with his stepfather. Stepfather forced Jack to play a waiter, the boy would run around and serve his stepfather, and if he refused, then the man would severely beat the kid. He slapped the kid's head and face with his open palm, there were no traces left, but this was very painful and offensive. Jack put a pot of water on the gas and covered it with a lid. Stepfather was drunk and dozing. Jack closed all the windows, and when the water boiled out of the pot and extinguished the fire, Jack left the house and went to see his mother in the hospital, so that no one would suspect him of participation in the death of his stepfather. Stepfather went to push daisies, and was peacefully buried in a deep hole. Jack lived a quiet life. But as it is inherent in every person, if there was an effective solution when a problem arose, this method of eliminating the calamity could always be applied. Jack liked to kill, and he could not stop himself until he met Cain. Jack was 16 then and calmly walked down the street thinking about how more money he needed to earn or steal to buy a car for his mother. He dreamed of buying a car for his beloved mother. A man was walking towards him. Jack sensed danger and wanted to cross the road, but felt dizzy, and stopped. In a split second, the man took him by the arm and said, "Do not be afraid, Jack, I will not harm you."

"Who are you?"

Jack's head was spinning and echoing.

"My name is Cain, and I will help you buy a car for your mom."

Jack did not believe anyone in his 16 years and did not believe in fairy tales either. He knew that the world was full of perverts and scoundrels, and everyone pursued his own interest only. He knew that no one helped anyone for no reason. Everyone looked for his benefit. Through the fog in his head, Jack reached into his pocket for his knife. He was about to pull out a knife and stealthily stab the good man in the stomach.

"Don't do that, Jack; your knife won't help you."

Then suddenly the fog clear away and clarity returned to Jack's head.

"What do you want?"

"Jack, you have killed your stepfather and three more people, and until now you are not under suspect, but if you don't stop, then charges could bc laid and the death penalty will be in store for you. You will be electrocuted after eight years. For six years in a row, you will be waiting for death in a condemned cell. I can show you this all."

Cain put his hand on the boy's shoulder, and Jack fell into a dream, where he saw his arms and legs tied up with straps, and someone pouring water on his head with a sponge... The fear overcame him, threw him into a cold sweat, and as if shocked, he came to his senses.

"Who are you?"

"I am Cain, I want to change your karma and give you a chance, God does not mind."

"You are like an angel or what?"

"Or what. I'm something else."

"Devil?"

"You won't guess, do not rake your brains, in proper time you will understand everything yourself."

"I want to buy a car for mom, I need a job."

"This is a piece of cake. Do you have a shovel at home?"

"Neighbor has."

"Go fetch the shovel, I'll show you something."

Jack was no longer hesitating, he trusted completely this stranger who knew absolutely everything about him. If he wished him bad, he would report on him to the police. Cain saw that Jack's eyes were clear and realized that he had become a father for Jack. Jack was looking for a father and found him. He ran up to Cain with a shovel in his hands.

"So, sir, what are we going to do?"

"We go for treasure hunting, then we buy a car for your mother."

"Oh, come on, sir," Jack smiled.

They walked along the road and went to 15 North Street.

"We go to the church, at the crossing with Sixth Avenue, see? This is a Baptist church, named after St. Paul."

Jack silently walked with a shovel on his shoulder, and nodded his head. There were trees growing along the road near the church. Cain crossed the road, came up to a certain tree and ordered Jack to dig. As soon as Jack just stuck a shovel into the soil, it immediately stumbled upon some object.

"What is there?"

"This is our treasure. There are two hundred thousand in a can."

"How do you know that?"

"I see a lot, there is a lot of money in the earth, people are burying for the future, but their future never comes. So there are the boxes left."

Jack dug the mud with his hands and pulled out an iron box from the ground. Jack's hands were shaking, he tried to open the box with his hands, but the lid rusted and sat tight. He fished for his switchblade, pulled it out of his pocket and began to pick the box. The lid bounced off and inside there were brand new dollars in a plastic bag.

"I cannot believe this!"

"This is for your living, Jack. Buy your mom a Cadillac for eighteen thousand, pay the rest of the money for the mortgage, buy everything you need for your house, buy new clothes and study well. I will watch you."

"But what should I do in exchange? What should I give you in return?'

"I need your friendship in return..."

"...A lot of water has flown under the bridge... And so here we are, sitting in the plane and drinking whiskey."

"Yes, Vassily. To be honest, it's best not to change anything. If God decided to send me to the electric chair, then so be it! Do not change fate. I would have been tried for four murders only, but now I have killed near a thousand people. I learned how to kill in different ways and I was paid for it and awarded with medals. The last medal I got from the president's hand personally. Then I murdered a whole village at once, I killed everyone, children, dogs and cats... And I was awarded for it, given a medal of honor and a watch. I wear it on my arm. So what's better? Be responsible for the death of four villains or for a thousand innocent souls? Probably I was cheated, and I will burn in hell. During the next thousand years they will kill me many times, so that I understand that one cannot consciously go against the Commandments of the Lord God. Thanks to Cain, he taught me everything..."

"Jack, listen, if a person was born in Africa, he had been no longer sinless, and if he were shot with a machine gun, then he was a hundred percent sinner. Otherwise, he would have been born white, in England, in the royal family. The main thing is that you began to understand the structure of the world, the existence of God and the Devil on the Earth, and learn much more, which you would never know. But for this knowledge you have to pay. You have already repented, you are not chasing medals, and you are already on the righteous path. Time to do good deeds, hope, and may God have mercy on you."

"You're still joking…"

"I also buggered up a lot, and made a heap of blunders, so what will happen to us? The bottle is already empty, but the conversation has just started!"

Vassily called the flight attendant, the plane had already reached the cruiser height and speed, and there was not much time left before the landing in Sochi. Cain had been looking out the window all the time and did not pay much attention to the conversation between Jack and Vassily. The flight attendant came over and brought a flight lunch, then treated the passengers with coffee and juice. Vassily began to consume the food enthusiastically, Cain languidly looked at him and offered him his portion, Vassily did not refuse, and devoured Cain's portion too. Having drunk in a gulp a whole glass of coffee with milk, Vassily continued his philosophical reflections.

"So it turned out that Cain has intervened in my case too. If he hadn't saved me and pulled me wounded out of the battlefield, I already would have been in Paradise, wouldn't make sins, and wouldn't kill people. And I had to kill not because of whim or pleasure; I was sent to war, and *à la guerre comme à la guerre*. Of course, I now think that if I understood better the Lord God's Commandments, then naturally I would have pretended to be demented, or would have refused to serve in the army altogether. I might even have been jailed for refusing to take   the oath of enlistment, but this all would be exactly better than blood on my hands."

Cain turned away from the porthole and it became clear from his face that he did not approve this conversation; he uttered words calmly, but with extraordinary force, **"Do you blame me for your sins? I can return the time back for each of you before meeting with me, you just ask and I will return you back to where I picked you."**

Jack and Vassily got frightened and sobered up right away.

Cain continued, "None of you approached God, none of you would know the Truth! You have learned the Truth thanks to me, the real Truth has been revealed to you, you know a lot about the Creator and you both are a thousand times smarter than any person on the Earth. You must pay a high price to get close to God and understand the meaning of life on the Earth. How many people do you know around you who possess this state of mind? Do you think the messengers of God do not kill people? They kill, and it is the will of the Lord God. If God wanted to change the fate of people, then THEY would change the trajectory of the planet by one angle degree, or bring the planet one step closer to the Sun. God desires to change everyone and what had happened to you was a learning process. And if you want to escape with a whole skin, then I can return you back."

Vassily's throat came sand-dry; he realized that Cain was very upset.

"Forgive me, I just said what I said. I'm glad I know you and glad that we are friends and I do not want to change anything. Brother, I am sorry; I did not want to upset you."

"You guys didn't upset me; I just am positive that people are not grateful. If someone does not like something, I can bring you back to your childhood any time and you will live without sin."

"My Lord, Cain, calm down, have I ever let you down? You are a father to me. Remember, I always do only what you order me. I have never failed you and never cheated."

"Jack, you could have become a saint, and I made a serial killer from you and now you will not get to Paradise. It is because of me that you will not be able to get to Paradise! I ruined all your life. Otherwise, you would be executed on the electric chair and God would send you to Paradise immediately, but now you will not see Paradise anymore!"

"Forgive me Cain, we were just shooting bull, I don't want to go to Paradise. I am happy with you; please don't get mad at us."

"If you guys cannot drink alcohol reasonably, then drink water, milk, or piss. Now the wine spirit clouds your minds, and your tongues are babbling uncontrollably. You have to ponder your every word and deed, have I really taught you otherwise?"

Suddenly a heavy nauseous odor of *The Roquefort Cheese*, unwashed body, stinking old rags, ammoniac and dirty sweaty socks stuffed the first-class compartment, and at the same time, the flight attendant announced the near destination landing in Sochi.

"What does it stink? Jack, are those your socks that stink so?"

"They ain't my socks!"

"Chill down, guys, it's just disgusting Kochenschwatz comes sneaky near. Back in '70s the communist leaders of the former USSR in commemoration of the 100th anniversary of Lenin's birthday produced the performances of an opera and then ballet 'October', where Vladimir Ilyich jumped around the stage in women's tights, and were about to launch a line of men's cosmetics and perfumes *The Odor of Ilyich*. What makes you so twitchy, you, castaway scum?"

"Dear Cain, I have been ordered to report on you, so I appeared."

"You appeared, and everything began to stink, there is nothing to report here, we just talk."

"I felt a conflict."

"No, there was just an intense conversation about the sense of life."

Jack and Vassily were no longer surprised that Cain was talking to himself. They knew that in this way he communicated with the spirits.

"So, shall I report that you have a problem with them?"

"You go ahead and report whatever you want, I will contact Archibald, and he will dump you back to your turdy whited sepulcher. Do not make me mad, otherwise I will finish your travels right now and here; I strongly advise you to do only what I order you. Then you can stay with me for a long time."

"Dear Cain, they stole your baggage. You are left without your suitcases."

"Who stole?"

"When sorting in Moscow; there is a gang of carriers operating there. They detected the money in your suitcase, your silver accessories, and Solomon's ring. You, Cain, live on the Earth for thousands of years, and still you are such a fool!"

"I have nothing to warry about, the one who had stolen, will bring everything to me and plead me on his knees to take it back. I am the right hand of the Devil, why should I warry about my junk? Do you know who stole?"

"Yes I know."

"So everyone knows. Report to Archibald immediately that my personal belongings were stolen by the villains and ask him to press the levers there."

"You got it!"

The lights turned on, they were landing, and everyone has fastened the seat belts.

In the meantime...

Archibald was sitting on the ocean beach looking at the sky. Suddenly the breeze brought the stench of old rags and sweaty socks, and Archibald grimaced.

"What do you want, Volodya?"

"I want to report that Cain had his suitcases stolen, and there all his personal belongings. He sent me to ask you make those villains bring the baggage to Abkhazia."

"Okay. Is that all?"

"Nothing else interesting."

"Fly back. I will solve the problem."

Archibald did not like scum tangling underfoot. He decided to stop and return back the time. He returned the moment of the baggage delivery. Archibald decided to attend and follow the suitcases in person. The man who scanned suitcases and bags was fingering for this gang. Before sending the baggage to the plane, this security officer x-rayed each suitcase and each bag. The state had created all this in order to control people totally. The man's name was Sidor, and now he stared at the monitor and at the same time evaluated the costly articles that were in each suitcase or bag. From each flight, he chose only one, maximum two suitcases.

Archibald appeared behind his back invisibly and just pushed him under his elbow; Sidor lost his balance and spilled his coffee on the keyboard. The coffee made a short circuit and the x-rays went out. Sidor could not help it, the baggage passed along the running tape, but the monitor did not show anything. Archibald was standing nearby; he knew absolutely everything about Sidor. He decided to contact his friend electrician, pulled a cell phone out of his pocket, but it was completely discharged. Sidor wondered what he should do; meanwhile the baggage was going along the treadmill without stopping. Two hours left until the end of the shift, during which time the device would not be repaired. He decided to seek help from the airport's technical support. The shift was lost in vain, that day he failed to steal anything. Sidor ran through the corridors, but there was no one at the airport, so he returned to his workplace. The carriers decided that he was deceiving them and stealing things for himself, they called him on his cell phone, but it was dead and off. They decided to punish him after work; they gave him a heavy thrashing, cleaned his pockets and dumped the crippled scoundrel in the street. Sidor died in a hospital of brain hemorrhage. Archibald was not to blame for the death of Sidor, he did not interfere in his fate; the thief was killed by his accomplices.

"The baggage is on the spot."

"Well, that's good."

Cain felt a burst of fire inside and realized that someone had paid for his suitcases with his life. Cain did not like dung flies. These little people without principles and fears, were sort of intrusive insects for him. As a rule, these souls have not yet passed enough trials and did not realize what could be stolen and what not.

They quietly landed in Sochi, passed the control without problems and took their belongings. Then they left the airport. There was already a minivan near the entrance. The airport was filled with Armenians. Armenians are a very ancient nation, just like the Semites and the Egyptians. They are divided into two castes, one caste are the noble, royal blood, and the other caste is mob, without principles and without morality. Naturally, the airport filled the majority of the second caste, which clang to visitors in hope to cheat money from them, offering their "priceless" services. Such a representative of the second caste, some Khachik Karapetian approached Cain.

"Eh, hello dear, where is we going? I know good hotel, not expensive!"

Cain looked at him with disgust.

"Look, Khachik. God doesn't love you, because THEY didn't create the man with the purpose to make the one like you! You have a very hard fate ahead, you smuggle drugs across the border and you will be imprisoned. You, Khachik, will serve eight years of strict regime. You will sit in Rostov, in the hut No 34 with the Cossacks; they will sod you and call you Khachik-Asshole-Doughnut-*Kalachik*!"

"Eh, who the hell is you? What is you saying? Tired of living? You is not driving from here, understand?"

"Now you complicate your life even more, I am a monk from the Orthodox Church, I will grind it into powder such a bedbug like you, want it? I do not believe that such Khachik-*Kalachik* descends from my parents Adam and Eve! God did not tell us everything; there must have been some kind of a stray dog tribe that had spawned!"

Vassily came close to Khachik, shoved a Glock 38 in his navel and in a sinistrous whisper told him, "Get the fuck out of here!"

Khachik looked down at his stomach, saw a gun that looked like a plastic toy pistol, thought that he was intimidated by a child's weapon and gained impudence.

"You is scaring me here with a baby gun? Who the fuck is you..."

He did not have time to finish the phrase, Vassily fired a shot and Khachik-*Kalachik* fell face down on the road. Two people in camouflage uniforms got out of the minivan and quickly approached Vassily.

"Wish health, Comrade Colonel, what to do with it?"

"Take this carrion to the hospital, and when he comes to senses, teach the scum to be afraid."

"Got it."

The military guys took the half dead typical representative of a proud Caucasian highland tribe by the legs and arms and dragged him to the bus. They dropped him like a bag of garbage on the asphalt. Opened the trunk and laid cellophane. Then they wrapped the unlucky body, and dumped it in the back of the bus. People silently observed this, nobody interfered, and the police as if did not exist. Everything was calm.

Cain arrived in Sochi. The beginning was not too bad, but promising.

"Tell me, Vasya, what for you have made a hole in him? Now this jerk has left on our bus."

"I could not help it. Forgive me Cain, I'll fix it right now."

"Come up to that guy with the beard, he has a normal car and he looks a cultured person. I have the impression that Archibald sent this bore to annoy us."

Cain shut his eyes and concentrated, but there was no answer.

"Volodya, where are you?"

Again the stench of old rags and *Roquefort* announced for everyone that the Communist Leader Lenin appeared nearby.

"Tell me, dear Ilyich, where is this shitty Khachik from?"

"I have no information yet; he was hanging around here every day. This was a trial from God. THEY wanted to test your patience and nobility."

"This is inappropriate, you cannot make me eat shit, and still smile broadly at the same time. I do not show nobility and patience in front of pigs. For in the Bible it is written in black on white, 'Give not that which is holy unto the dogs, neither cast ye your pearls before swine, lest they trample them under their feet, and turn again and rend you.' I am also an active element of the Orthodox Church. I should have at least minimal respect. Therefore, I passed the test. Especially since I did not shoot, but my friend. Although, I don't argue, if I had a gun, I would shoot him right in the head and that Khachik-*Kalachik* would roll to hell by a straight path. But my faithful friend Vassily gave this scoundrel a chance to step on the path of correction. So, as always, I'm doing everything right!"

Vassily came up to Cain along with the young man, whom Cain had noticed earlier, and pointed to him.

"Hello, my name is David, I can deliver you anywhere in the vicinity at a reasonable price."

"David, who are you by nationality?"

"I am Armenian."

"It is amazing how this world is fascinatingly arranged, dear David. I need to go to Abkhazia, to New Athos. How much is it?"

"As I see, you are a priest or a monk. I am ready to drive you to New Athos free, provided that you refill my gas tank. I am a believer and used to be often in Mount Athos at the Divine Service. Now, I live like everyone else. Therefore, I will gladly go with you and deliver you to the Temple of the Lord."

"Attaboy! Look, Vassily, this is how a decent person should talk. You have a noble name, David. Do you read the Bible? I knew David personally; he was a crazy guy, but righteous and devoted to God. And this is the most important thing, the rest is not important."

"So, friends, come on, let's drive."

All quickly followed David with their baggage. David had a comfortable Japanese minivan. Jack was the last to go; he looked down under his feet and was plunged in deep thought about something.

"Jack, my dear friend, why are you so upset?"

"I did not have time to protect you, I did not understand anything. I don't know Russian and therefore I did not know that this bastard insulted you. I would kill him too. But it happened so, as if I pissed my pants and did not react."

"My dear Jack, don't you know that I can mentally give you a command? Or do you think that I do not know what kind of person you are? I take only brave, valiant, honest, and infinitely courageous people as my friends and you are my family. I am able to protect myself, and you, and even return you from the netherworld. And I know that you will jump after me into the abyss without hesitation, I see your brave and honest heart, so do not be sad, my brother. We arrived in a sunny city; enjoy it, everything will be fine.”

“Thank you, Boss for trusting me, next time give me a sign, and don’t dump me in a foolish situation.”

“Okay, Jack.”

All settled in a comfortable Japanese minivan and set off towards the Abkhaz border. “Forgive me my interest, friends; I see a foreigner among you, and do you have Abkhaz visas?”

“We are personnel of the Ministry of Communications; we can go without permits.”

“I just want us to pass the border without any problems.”

Vassily was talking on the phone all the time.

“Vassily, let’s bet, that I will cross two borders without any document.”

“I know your ways. You scramble a man’s brains and start to manage him; I saw it.”

“Okay, since you saw it, I won’t. And we can also contact Archibald and report to him that we cannot pass the border... Then we’ll see what he would do, I wonder. Archibald always has fresh ideas, like, for example with suitcases, when he deftly returned my suitcases to the flying plane. I am delighted, no one magician in the world can perform this!”

“How did he do it? It took him only several minutes. How can one return the suitcases to a flying plane in counted minutes?”

“This was a mere trifle for him, he had returned time back, and that was it. For him, time is like a thought, he thinks, and time moves in any direction. For him no concept of time exists. Time was invented for people to go to work. Otherwise time does not exist, for him precisely, time does not exist.

Vassily smiled and said, “Holy Father, do not trouble the Devil, I have arranged everything, they are already waiting for us.”

“Oooh! Vassily, I see you are ready to come to me for the confession, I will be happy to grant you absolution and bless you!”

“Cai, you anyway know everything about me.”

They arrived to the state border and stopped in front of the barrier, a man approached the van. Vassily opened the door, the man saluted and said, “Prepare any documents you have.”

Cain pulled out his diplomatic passport; Vassily prepared a certificate for Jack and his service certificate. The man got in their van.

"You drive right there!" David silently drove past all cars in a queue; a border guard blocked the road.

"Wish health, where are you going?"

Vassily's acquaintance rolled down the side window, and said, "These people are with me."

The border guard recognized the officer, saluted and said, "Drive right through!"

Cain thought that most people live and do not know that there is a certain level, where they do not need visas, documents, and different permits.

Cain could not bother at all, fly by his personal plane and land in Sukhumi, or in Sochi, and then fly by helicopter to New Athos. And there was no need in any documents, visas or permits. Or he could summon demons, and teleport in a second anywhere in the world, along with his suitcases. Cain raised most of the oligarchs and politicians; Cain created banks and money, together with Archibald. The Rockefellers, Rothschilds and Morgans were his children. Archibald personally invented the banking system *Morgan GP* to enslave peoples. The banks initiate and provoke massive sins, deceptions, thefts, lies, robberies and murders. Archibald controls all this den, the Devil gives loans, and then takes away the holy soul from people; this is what any bank does. This is the Devil's most deft invention, his jewelry craft; a self-destroying system that moves everyone away from God. Archibald manages banks, banks rule the world, and no politician can change this. Cain can do absolutely everything that comes into his head boundlessly, because the banks control everything and everybody, governments, ministers and presidents. Therefore, Cain did not give a damn for rules and laws. He created all the laws, The Code of Hammurabi, Roman law and constitutions. So Cain just fooled along; he simply wanted to have a ride and look at people and customs. But people do not know that they all are sheep and behind them is a shepherd who herds, milks, and eats them.

The van drove up to the Abkhaz border. David came to life and without any instructions passed over all cars, and stopped near the border guard.

"Hello Adgur, here are people from the ministry."

The man in gray, a friend of Vassily, went out and began to explain something. Another border guard approached and a minute later the man in gray sat back in the van and said, "Everything is okay, let's move."

David knew that he could drive faster than normal; he realized that he was traveling with powerful people who were above the law. But David did not know too much. Vassily patted him on the shoulder and said, "Come on, buddy, floor it to Athos. On the way, pull over somewhere to take a snack; we arrived in the country of the Soul, Apsny!"

"There are many cafes on the way there."

"Abkhazia is a land blessed by God. There are no generally accepted rules and laws. Here they do not know this exotic word 'constitution'! What is *constitution*?"

Jack entered the conversation.

"Tell me, what is this country and whose cows lie on the road?"

"These are sacred cows; they came from India and stayed here. God first created Abkhazia, and then many thousands of years later created your America with *Mac Donald's*! They say that Adam and Eve lived in Abkhazia, and then God expelled them, because they did not want to obey."

"Vassily, take a break."

"Well, Cain, okay, tell us the story of Abkhazia."

"I don't know; I've never been here. David, you tell the story of Abkhazia."

"Abkhazia is an ancient state. Archaeological discoveries indicate the presence of man on the territory of Abkhazia, even in the era of the Lower Paleolithic, approximately 300-400 thousand years ago."

"Oho, I did not know that; so what's happened next?"

"Then the Greeks came, brought their culture. The capital was Sukhumi, and the Greeks called it Dioscuriad. Dio is God. Then the Romans came and renamed the capital Sebastopolis. And already in the fourth century AD, Abkhazia became part of the Byzantine Empire, and it were they, who, around the sixth century A.D., brought Christianity to Abkhazia. In the sixth century, the formation of an independent Abkhazian kingdom began, which also included western Georgia. So the capital was Athos, and then in 800, the capital of the Abkhaz kingdom was Kutaisi."

"Wow, I did not know that the Abkhazian kingdom included a part of Georgia! Yes, I am not much of a history lover; I thought that Abkhazia used to be part of Georgia. That's all I knew."

"The Abkhazian kingdom was for a long time self-governing and independent state. Then the Ottoman Empire obtained an imposing influence, and some Abkhazians accepted Islam. The Abkhazians wanted to get out of the influence of Turkey and formed an alliance with the Russian Empire. Approximately, in 1800, the manifesto of Alexander I about the annexation of Abkhazia to Russia was issued. They wanted to enslave Abkhazians and introduce serfdom, half the population were killed treacherously by the Russian troops, part of the Abkhazians fled to Turkey. When the Abkhaz population declined, Mingrelians and Georgians began to arrive in Abkhazia. This happened around 1870 when Georgians filled Abkhazia. Many Abkhazians were bound to leave their homeland and flee to Turkey. In 1917, the Communists came to power. In 1920, Abkhazia became part of the Georgian Soviet Socialist Republic, in 1922 the Abkhaz Autonomous Soviet Socialist Republic was formed."

"Okay, now I see. Very interesting, I did not know that. Well done David, but how do you know this? You're not an Abkhazian, are you? I thought that the Abkhazians were a tribe that, together with the Russian troops, conquered part of the territory from Georgia and arbitrarily called themselves Abkhazia. But it turns out that everything is vice versa and much more complicated..."

"My ancestors lived here, and therefore, it was always interesting for me to know my history. Abkhazians are an ancient culture, such as Armenians and Greeks."

"So they observe no official rules here?"

"The community have always decided here, here the community decide the fate of each person according to tradition. Abkhazians do not want to see strangers in command here, which always ended badly."

"Does this concern us?"

"No, it concerns profiteers and hucksters."

"I have never been a huckster; we are not profiteers, so there will be no problems. I understand why there is a permanent war for this territory; there is a very beautiful nature here, clear sea, and breathtaking mountains."

David looked at the road and said, "Freshwater here is the most delicious in the world!"

"Let's make a stop, have a snack, and try this sweet water."

They drove up to Gagra. On the way, they stopped at a diner. David asked to treat the guests with national dishes and drinks, asked for fresh water. Cain did not eat anything; he nourished otherwise, but decided to try the water.

"Delicious water. I think that local enterprisers would be able to sell such water for export throughout the whole world. This is a more profitable business than oil trading. Water is necessary for everyone; people are made of water, so water is the most important element. Polluted water causes diseases and mental disorders. People do not completely understand the importance of clean water. Stupid people can pay a thousand dollars for a bottle of champagne, but they don't want to pay reasonable price for a glass of clean fresh water. After all, what benefits them is of little interest to them. People think that filtered water of the second cycle is the same as spring water. All diseases begin from the water supplied by the dirty pipes in megalopolises. Nevertheless, people are not interested in a healthy lifestyle. In ancient times, spring water, over which prayers were pronounced, was called 'live water'. And this is not a falsehood. People have forgotten the ability to change the structure of matter with a word. Each person can heal himself or change himself by prayer or certain word combinations. The word, like a key, cuts into the ether and selects the necessary combinations with vibrations. Therefore, ancient people, before consuming water or food, prayed and asked the Lord God to bless their meal. And those who cooked food for their kings and at the same time cursed mentally or with words the prepared food or water, created 'dead' water and 'deadly' food."

"It sounds like a fairy tale about magicians and wizards."

"No, it's true, take two glasses of water, read prayers over one, and utter cursing words over another glass. Then put both glasses in the freezer and when the water freezes, you will see smooth snowflakes in the glass over which beautiful prayers were read, and tattered and ugly patterns in the other glass over which evil words were spoken."

"Wow, I'll check it!"

"Go ahead; with a word, you can either heal, or kill. If people knew that, they would not use venoms and weapons."

"Yes, for this they will not be able to convict you! Cool to be able to do so!"

"Anyone can do it, you just need to be cleansed of filth and feel the fire inside, but it is fraught with danger. THEY can punish you for this and it is easier to receive punishment from people than from God. People have no imagination, but God knows how to punish severely. Mark you, that a criminal after prison very often repeats crimes, but if God punishes, then a hundred percent there would be no relapse."

After the delicious lunch, they got into the van and moved on towards New Athos.

Cain dozed off, it happened rarely, but he always had colorful and very realistic visions, as this time. He dreamed that they were driving along the main road to Abkhazia. David calmly accelerated, suddenly the car jerked sharply to the right, and David tried to turn the steering wheel so that the car would not slide on the shoulder of the road. The car turned around, and it began to move against the traffic, oncoming cars tried to avoid collision and drove off the road. David hit the brake and the car stopped.

"Praised be God!"

"Do not praise God, it is to commemorate the Lord in vain."

"Well, let's say, I do not consider this a common situation. I thank God that I remained intact, we are all alive, and the car is undamaged. So thank you, Lord!"

Cain looked at the joyful David and said nothing. The right back tire had busted, Jack pulled out the spare tire and waited for David to give him the wrench to change the wheel. David walked around the car and was as happy as a child; he pulled out a wheel wrench and a tire jack. Jack showed by facial expression that he would change the wheel himself. David lit a cigarette; he was in a great mood.

"What do you smoke, grandson?"

David turned around and saw a very old woman with worn packages and plastic bags in her hands; she looked horrible.

'A poor homeless woman,' David thought, 'pity for that grandmother.'

"Greetings, Granny, how can I help you?"

"Oh, grandson, I have to go to Athos, give me a lift!"

"Granny, I don't go myself; if my passengers agree, then I don't mind either."

David approached Cain:

"Holy Father, can we take this grandma with us? We're going the same way."

"Let her go with us, I do not mind, settle her."

David ran to the old woman and said, "I'll put your things in the back, choose and sit yourself wherever you want."

"Thank you good boy, God help you."

The grandma put her old bags and worn packages in the trunk, then pushed the door back and climbed into the van. Vassily sat in his place by the window and asked, "Good day, grandma, where are you heading?"

"Let me take your seat near the window, sonny, make room for me, I want to sit there. It's a long way, so I need a good place."

Vassily thought that the grandma was whimsy, but then he reflected on life and mentally agreed that Granny lived a hard life, so now she has the right to demand the best place. Meanwhile, Jack has changed the tire, David finished his cigarette, and everyone climbed back into the van. Jack glanced at the old lady, but said nothing. All were silent; David looked at the road and drove in compliance with the rules of the traffic, not exceeding the speed limit.

"Well done grandson, follow the rules!"

Cain lurked and felt an incomprehensible uneasiness; he began to examine the old woman. Were it Archibald, Cain would immediately feel his presence. Cain wrapped his mind around this grandma. Something was wrong with her. He knew there are no coincidences in life, which meant that the old woman planned to bust the tire, in order to go with them to Athos. Where did she come from? Grandma looked in the window and mumbled something. No one understood anything. Vassily looked at the old woman and asked, "Granny, what village are you from?"

"I come from Germany; I reached the mountain passover during the war and stayed here. My brother and I grew up in an orphanage in Berlin. My brother's name was Rudolph. Then Rudolph disappeared, they took him to a special school, and I remained in the orphanage."

Vassily came out of relaxed state and intently looked at the old lady.

"Are you German?"

"Yes, I used to be German. Then I studied at the Faculty of Biology and in 1939, they included me in the *Ahnenerbe* project. I was searching for my lost brother everywhere, but never found him."

Vassily got into a stupor and asked, "I missed something, how old are you now?"

"You have problems with math, son? Count! So this is where I lead, many years I look for this kind man who took my Rudolph from me..."

Cain did not listen to what the grandma told Vassily. He knew that grandma was with a catch. And he did not like catches and surprises. Through the noise of the car, music and conversations came the words of the grandma, "...and the time was hungry, we were not fed at all in the orphanage. We thought that we would die of hunger and suddenly a man came, very nicely dressed and we knew that he was rich. He brought a lot of food for us children and for the teachers too... We could hardly believe our happiness... My brother Rudolph made a wire hoop over his head with antennas... I then asked him, why he was wearing this hoop wire with horns... And he told me, my Margo, this is so that God can hear us better... This is an amplifier for my prayer... As this kind rich man heard those words, he burst into tears... He could not stop, and after that, we had everything in the orphanage and my brother Rudolph lived better than anyone else did..."

Cain jumped up and jerked the grandma by the collar with all his might.

"Who are you, old bitch? Speak, otherwise I will tear you into pieces! Jack, Vassily, give me the gun! Who are you, witch?"

Grandma smiled and took Cain by the hand.

"Aha, now you remember little Margo?"

"Who the hell are you?"

David pulled over to the shoulder and stopped the car. Jack wanted to pull the gun out of the holster, but the body did not obey him.

Suddenly the old woman's attitude changed, her eyes glittered and the granny continued in a loud and clear voice, "Cain, regards from Margot, remember her? All her life, until her death, she was looking for you and her brother. I felt sorry for them and helped them meet."

"Raphael? And I was racking my brain to guess who was this merry old lady? Therefore, I could not understand anything. Did THEY send you for my soul?"

"No, what made you think so?"

"Well, THEY usually sent you for a soul; you are the punishing power of the Lord of the Worlds!"

"Actually, yes, you are right, but not this time. THEY know that you have repented long ago and helped many people to get close to God and therefore I arrived here with the aim to convey the message. THEY want you to stop yourself. You must comprehend personally that the virus that you create will not change anything. Are you ready to risk your immortal soul?"

"I will not live here anymore, I hate people and I hate the Earth, I have had enough of it! I will finish what I have planned, and if you intend to kill me, then do it now!"

"No. I have no right to kill you. Remember, we are watching you; you will perish in torments like everyone else. You will not have protection this time. You will be responsible for every soul, and you know what a projection is?"

"Yes, projection is the future of each person."

"Therefore, you do not know the future, even the most dreadful demon can become a believer devoted to God, say, in a year or ten years from now. Are you sure you will kill the right people or you want to add worries THEM with your insane actions?"

"Kill me now and finish it all! Kill me and burn my soul!"

Cain shouted loudly in his sleep, Vassily tried to wake gently his boss and best friend.

"Cain, wake up, wake up!"

Vassily pinched Cain's hand.

"Where am I?"

Vassily took Cain by the hand and calmly replied, "We go to New Athos."

"Yeah, well, I dreamed about all this nonsense. Did I say something?"

"Yes, you shouted... 'burn my soul!'"

"Clear. How much left to go, David?"

"I hear you Holy Father, we have about forty minutes, maybe an hour."

"Is there a hotel?"

"Yes, there is a hotel *Owl*, cute, comfy and near the sea."

"Well, first we go to the monastery, and then we settle in the *Owl*."

Cain reflected on his dream and realized that it was not a dream, and that Archangel Raphael was really talking to him. Cain thought. 'It means that I am on the right path, since one of the first Archangels of the Lord God has descended to me. It makes no sense to stop, THEY know that I have already repented many times, and have cleared myself; I am ready for any outcome of my existence. I am tired.

Time passed quickly, and soon they entered Athos.

 "Here we are, on the spot."

David turned off the main road and began to ascend to the New Athos temple.

David proceeded his historical review.

"This temple was founded in the 1800 s, it was completely built in 1875 by the hands of Russian monks with the sponsoring of the Russian Emperor Alexander III. It is not a matter of historical facts, but of the place itself. The land on which the monastery is built possesses immense magic power and only the elected know this. Sins are absolved here, contracts are concluded between Heaven and the Earth. Not everyone can go up to the temple."

"Interesting," Cain said.

David's van climbed up '*the long and winding* mountain *road*' and he parked it on the small lot. The view was beautiful, the sky merged with the sea, and on the other side blue mountains towered over them. While travelers got out of the passenger compartment and began to look around, Cain thought about how to find Seraphim and called the Leader of the world lumpen-proletariat.

"I listen obediently, my dear Master Cain."

"How far do I have to go to Seraphim and what is needed for this?"

"I advise you to meet Hieromonk Grigori and visit Seraphim jointly."

"Does he believe in God?"

"Yes, he does, very honestly!"

"Well, so why the hell do I need him then?"

"He will not detect you, tell him your legend, give him some money for repairing the temple, and he will go anywhere with you. The main thing is to show him the money and donate a certain sum; they started renovation there in the temple, but desperately lack money."

"Call him out, I am coming."

"He will be waiting for you right at the entrance to the temple."

Life in the temple was going calmly and evenly. Peace of mind and complete tranquility of heart is what Our Lord bestows on people if they desire to get at least one step closer to Him.

Father Grigori decided to look around and check the tidiness and order in the yard. And all of a sudden, an unknown monk, or a priest appeared in front of him. He was unlikely a priest, too humble and modest his attire for a priest was, no gold cross, worn and even shabby cassock. Looked like a monk from afar whom a brisk need ended up there.

"May God be with you!" The unknown monk said.

"Good day to you, Reverend, how can I help you?"

"Oh, yes, Father Grigori, you can help me, I would like to go about the holy places of pilgrims."

"Very good, but where are you from?"

"Oh, I am from far away, the Kaluga Diocese! I presume you have heard of such an Optina Desert. Of a small town of Kozelsk?"

"Yes of course I know. Where are you staying?"

"I have stayed yet nowhere, I have just arrived and would like to look around, I would like to visit the Holy Sermon and visit all the holy places."

"Now I will order to set the table. You can stay with us, we have a lot of space here, and there would be enough food for everyone. We have started renovation now, we will complete the repair and then it would be possible to accommodate the pilgrims."

"I would like to help you in your noble deed."

"Yes, thank you, we do everything ourselves with our own hands."

"I would like to make a donation to your temple, if you do not mind."

"God forbid, I do not!"

Cain pulled out a thick afore-prepared wad of euros. Grigori's thoughts confused, he raked his brain, why did this poor monk suddenly decided to give a fortune to their church. Wasn't he the Devil in the flesh? Probably the Devil, only the Devil makes such gifts. So here, Grigori decided not to take the money in his hands and tried to play smart.

"Aha, and what's your name, Reverend? You did not introduce yourself."

"I am Nikon."

"Well, well, I am afraid there is no one under the name of Nikon there."

"But you can call them; nothing easier – there is a telephone in the monastery."

"This is all the tricks of the Devil! What night prayer do you read?"

Cain could not restrain himself and began to smile.

"I read such prayers as all the believers do. The *Lord's Prayer*, the *Jesus's Prayer* and to the *Holy Mother of God*."

Grigori looked at the stranger and thought:

'No, he is not the Devil, he calmly speaks about prayers, and he knows the names of the prayers. Why did these thoughts come to my mind that I think badly of the man?'

"My brother Nikon, welcome, my home is your home. You can count on me, I will help you with all your needs, I can take you to all holy places, and we will pray together."

"Perfect. Take the alms, do not hesitate."

"That's a lot of money, where did you get it from?"

"In this case, a sinner came to our monastery and solicited my sympathy with his talks and repentance, and then asked me to confess him."

"So, he donated this cash?"

"Yes, he told me, he had earned all this money sinfully, and they were a burden to him. So he decided to allocate all his money to the temple and to me personally. Thus, I distribute it."

"But you are a noble servant of the Lord God."

"God sees us all, and that cannot be any other way, this money, they are like hot tar, I cannot use it for my own purposes. I should quickly distribute them and take off this responsibility."

"Did you not think of giving everything to a charitable foundation?"

"No, any such fund is a hoax. They are servants of the Devil, and they misappropriate the money for themselves. Here, you need twenty thousand euros to complete this wing, this will be sufficient for the material, the new windows and doors."

"How can you know that?"

"When I stood below, I heard a conversation between two old women. Your parishioners also know about your problems."

"And, indeed, I said this in the service of God."

"You see, and you all suspect me of something unseemly."

"You are a very mysterious character for me, and your modesty and the gratuitous generosity of yours reminded me of the Devil. The old writings often described the

Devil in human flesh; even writers such as Goethe also tried to describe the Devil in detail. I know that he exists and can adopt any shape."

"Nonsense, Holy Father. What can the Devil do without the highest permission of the Lord God? And if you are tempted, then, what the Devil has to do with it? Everyone blames the Devil; but does the Devil force them to do something? Everyone wants a luxurious car, a bigger house, a lot of money, power, and they have to pay for all this. Is it not so written in the Bible?"

"But not everyone reads the Bible."

"Does everyone read the criminal code?"

"No, as for me, I have not read it."

"Therefore, if you have not read the criminal code and do not know the laws, then you would not be judged if you commit a crime?"

"No, ignorance of the laws is no excuse."

Grigori smiled generously; he realized that the guest knew all the laws very well.

"Indeed, you are a very interesting person; people of such thinking and attitude towards the world are rarely met. You have a good understanding of the world order; allow me to ask you, how old are you?"

"I am 45."

"I can always determine the age, but in your case I am confused, the expression of your face is like that of an old wise man, but the skin is young, sporty, I don't understand it, my brother Nikon!"

"True, everybody says that to me, in my family all were clerics and I have been reading the Bible already from childhood, I learned it by heart, I can recite any page from the Holy Letter from my memory. I mean primarily the Old Testament, because the New Testament, the Gospel is very confusing. The Gospel was not written for me, although I read and studied it.

"Why? You don't believe in Christ, Brother Nikon?"

"I do, but I've read some other Revelations, little known, and they do not coincide."

"Oh yes, they are known to me. So what?"

"So the fact is, my dear Brother Grigori, that the Truth is one and only, and there may be no more versions. When people lie, then there are the versions first, second and tenth. But the Truth is always the same. Say, you read the Old Testament; it has no versions, the Jews adopted the Old Testament, like the Torah, that is, the Pentateuch of Moses."

"Well, unfortunately, one life is not enough to delve into it, we still cannot change anything."

"I cannot agree with you, my Brother Grigori, every person says so and eventually everyone goes the wrong way. The fate of total humankind lies in the hands of every single person. Every person, even humble, poor, or unemployed, has a connection with God, and every person influences the fate of humanity. After all, God gives everyone as he needs; and if a person does not want anything, then God does not give anything. *Inactivity* is the gravest sin; when you see a crime or a lie and do nothing to avert it, then you automatically become an accomplice of lies and crimes."

"Well, I do not agree. Say, a villain comes to power somewhere in Africa; he has the power and the army. What can a common man change?"

"Every African resident is worthy a ruler whom he deserves. Look, for example, in your country, when the Russian Tsar wanted to introduce serfdom in Abkhazia, nobody wanted to become a slave, so he killed nearly everyone. Now, they are free in Paradise, with God, and the slaves on the Earth worship their dictators. That is the difference. What does Judaism or Islam teach? They teach freedom and independence! Moses led three generations of Jews in the wilderness of the desert to convert them from Egyptian slaves into free masters, born to rule other nations. Moses remade their DNA; he weaned the Jews away from slave hand labor and taught them to work with their minds only. Only when you work with your brain, and not with your hands, you can earn a comfortable worthy life. That was Moses's aim and achievement. A lot of people hate the Jews for this, but they stealthily and steadily rule dissatisfied masses. This is their culture, they do not give up and do not turn away from their kin, they give work only to their coreligionists and relatives, the synagogue unites them and the rabbi, who prompts and reminds them each time the Law of Moses. But among Christians, there are no such rules, and when there is no unity, it is easy to kill such a community one by one, they can easily be manipulated. They are like sheep without a shepherd, they wander by themselves, they are beaten, they are made into burgers and eaten. But the Jews are a pack of wolves, they are few, but they work as a united organism, as one whole. For their convenience, they came up with Christianity as a religion for slaves."

"Nikon, what are you talking about? We are not slaves!"

"You are not a slave, but those who worship Christ and the Crucifix are slaves."

"It's not true what you say! You cannot say that!"

"Oh, yes! This is a secret! I forgot, but we know *the truth*, don't we?"

"Where from such thoughts come to your mind?"

"Did you compare the Old Testament and the New Testament, Reverend? These are two books, that contradict each other; but Jesus said that he agreed with the teachings of the previous prophets. It turned out that he agreed, but taught his disciples something different."

"You misunderstood everything."

"I understood correctly, because I know the Truth! God is One, and God created a free man, not a slave. Therefore, if a person voluntarily becomes a slave, it means that Lucifer was right when he did not bow to the man; if a man is a slave it means that he has another master besides the Lord God. Lucifer disobeyed God, for which he was punished; but God sees that people have become stupid and ungrateful."

Grigori was scared, and his heart sank; he felt a fever for no reason, he began to choke and thought that he needed to go inside and wash himself with cold holy water.

"Dear Brother Nikon, let's go to our table; you, brother, need to eat after the road, and have a rest."

"First I will check in the hotel because I am not alone, and then I will find you here; we need to discuss a lot of questions."

Father Grigori wanted to say goodbye to his guest as soon as possible, he was in a fever, and he felt how the ground receded from under his feet.

"Now, I have to go, dear Nikon I am waiting for you, come at any time, I will aid you, and do whichever is in my power."

Cain smiled, the beginning was not bad; this Father Grigori will be with him, and will help him, this was a good news. Cain went back to the van; David stood near it.

"Tell me, dear David, do you have a dream?"

"I dream a lot, someday I will build a house or a hotel, I will definitely set up a big garden, I will grow tangerines, nuts, maybe I will make a greenhouse, then I will be calm. Then I could die in peace knowing that my children have a shelter over their heads."

"Have you ever calculated how much money you need?"

"In dollars, that would be not less than one hundred thousand. I will build brick by brick, but I will build a large house, independent, with my own well, solar panels and sewage system, so that not to pay anything to anybody."

"Have you already been in the temple?"

"No, first I will check you in a hotel, and then I will go and pray."

"Now look, you will go to a normal bank, to the *Raiffeisen Bank*, you will find the manager and show him the check, do not show it to the operators, they will not know what to do with it."

Cain pulled out a pen, scratched a few lines in his checkbook and handed the check to David. David picked it up and looked at the check. An amount of one hundred thousand dollars was signed out there.

"Dreams come true David, if you want your children to be happy, pray, and make your entire family pray, pray sincerely and earnestly. Faith will soon be very useful to for you to survive in the literal sense."

David was astonished, he could not move, and stood still like a monument. It was a strong shock for him; he knew that he was not being cheated and that his dream had come true. David began to ponder, and thought that he needed money for gas to return to Sochi, and he decided for himself that he would donate exactly half of that money to the temple.

"Oh, you probably need money to return to Sochi, here, take five hundred euros, change, and refuel. Mind, that the money that I gave you is all yours. Do not give it to anyone; otherwise, you will never build your house. Today I have already given Father Grigori money for the temple. Remember, this money is yours, start building a house and pray!"

David did not know what to say. He lit a cigarette to calm himself down. Cain saw the cigarettes and said, "If you smoke, God will not see you through the smoke. Do not smoke, David. The Devil invented tobacco in order to distance man from God. Remember my words; I know what I am talking about."

David dumped a cigarette and trampled it down with his sole, then quickly picked up the crushed butt, and put it in his pocket.

"Over there is a garbage can; throw everything in the trash so as not to stink. God does not love the weak and smelly. Memorize that."

"I will remember your words, Holy Father."

"My name is Cain, for all the others I am Father Nikon, understand?"

"Yes, Father Nikon, I will remember."

"Where are the rest people?"

"They went downhill to see the waterfall."

"Go and fetch them, we need to check into the hotel."

"Can I ask you a question?"

"Go ahead."

"If I could, in gratitude for your gift, stay with you and help you with everything to finish your plans."

"If you want, you can stay. Gather everyone; we have to go. We are short of time."

"I run."

David ran down the road to the waterfall.

Cain looked at the sky and pondered. Ten minutes later, his real friends were ascending the road. Cain realized that they could not survive the virus and this virus would inevitably kill them. He knew that cruel punishment awaited them, and that THEY would retaliate them for their sins, and there would be no forgiveness for them.

<u>Because God is not a kind grandfather who forgives everything and everyone, God is justice, God is a scale and everyone pays for what he takes and does.</u>

The guys cheerfully ran up to the minivan. Vassily looked at Cain and asked, "Well, did you succeed?"

"Yes, we have acquitted a good assistant. David, now let's go to the hotel."

"That is good, and who is it?"

"Reverend Grigori."

"Bribetaker with itchy palms, and a parasite?"

"No, he is on the righteous path and he will improve. He will help us. I gave him hot tar; this is money for the temple renovation. If he steals at least one *kopeck* from this money, he undoubtedly will be immediately punished. Demons stand on watch of his every step. It will happen to him as described in the Holy Qur'an.

<u>"Surely the tree of the Zaqqum,</u>

<u>Is the food of the sinful</u>

<u>Like dregs of oil; it shall boil in (their) bellies,</u>

<u>Like the boiling of hot water."</u>

"What is this tree like?"

"This is a bitter tree without fruits, which causes unbearable torments to the human soul. First, I will send him troubles in life, and then we will punish him even after death."

"Do you think he knows that you are checking on him?"

"I believe that he is more a decent man rather than he is a grabber."

They all got into a minivan and headed to the *Owl Hotel*. This hotel stood right on the sea beach.

"David, do you know anybody in this hotel? Here the gate seems closed and the door too."

"We have just to call and they will open."

David got out of the car and went to the intercom.

"Here are guests to you, open up."

The gate has opened.

Cain looked at Vassily and Jack and said, "You both guys sit here, I myself will look around, and if it's normal, then we check in."

"You got it, Boss."

Cain got out of the car and followed David inside. The place was small; everything was small, but cozy and clean.

"Do you have a room with a sea view?"

"Yes, will you settle in?"

"I will."

"Well, I'll prepare the rooms for you, how many places do you need?"

"I need three rooms, each with a large bed and with all the conveniences; the sea view is relevant only for me."

"For how long are you planning to stay?"

"A week, not more."

"Seven days, three rooms with double beds, is that correct?"

"Yes, count the cost and I will immediately pay. Breakfast included?"

"Yes, breakfast is until ten in the morning, a buffet."

"Fine, show our suites, please, we are checking in. David, call the guys, let them come here with the baggage."

"Father Nikon, and where am I supposed to live?"

"You go home, David, get busy with your plans."

"However, dear Father Nikon, without a car it would be rather difficult for you to solve your problems. I will call my wife and she will understand. I may stay with you and help you. Moreover, the payment here is only in *rubles*."

"If you want, stay, I'll show you something, and you will understand everything at once."

Cain approached the administrator, looked into his eyes intently and said, "I paid for the rooms, I gave you the money, where is my change?"

"Oh, excuse me, I forget, but what is the rest? How much do I owe you?"

"You must give me all the cash you have."

"Okay, I'll fetch everything right now."

David was shocked; he had never seen such impudent tricks.

"Do you think, David, I need this money? I can make everyone come to us, give everything to the last *kopeck*, and do what I command him. But I am not interested. I want to punish this guy because he steals. He misappropriates most of the income."

The manager ran down the hallway. In his hand he had money, squeezed into a fist.

"Not a lot of money here, the income is too small."

Cain took the manager by the shoulder and said:

"We paid you for our stay, but you were robbed. Remember, two people came down from the sky and aimed a space weapon at you, they took all the proceeds, and flew off into the sky."

"Yes, I was robbed, I am very sorry."

"Now give us the keys to the entrance doors and to the suites, and go to sleep."

"Yes, here are your keys and a magnetic master key, take it and I go to bed."

The administrator placed the money on the table and put the keys on it.

"You are free, get out of here."

The administrator turned round and left.

"Why didn't you do this to me?"

"Because you truly believe in God, and you are not a rotten person yourself, I see you through. You are just a normal honest man. And your family is not bad, you were brought up correctly, taught not to lie and not to cheat and not to steal. This is already a lot."

"Clear, and you see all people like that?"

"Yes. I can also call any lost soul and ask if I'm not sure about something."

"Do you do magic?"

"Magic is the knowledge, and God gives knowledge and skills."

"Did God teach you to induce people into hypnosis and extort money from them?"

"I don't need money, and God knows it, I just sometimes put people in their right place. This administrator is a scoundrel and I simply punished him."

"I understand, thank you for helping and not punishing me. I am not a saint either."

"Yes, but your sins are mere harmless trifles. I know everything."

"Thank you."

"Thank God, you should thank God for everything that happens to you. If other people help you, it means that God sent them to you. There are no other options. If you were robbed, then God did it to bring you to reason or teach you a lesson. Man is born rich or poor, God decides it, man dies rich or poor, God decides it too. Everything is decided only by God, the Creator of the worlds, God decides the existence of different galaxies and the life of each creature. God is an immense Power and Energy Who decides the fate of all things. If you do something wrong or say a stupidity, you kindle God's anger, and change your fate instantly. The gravest sin is blasphemy. If a person in his stupidity believes that he is a god, then he is a dead meat and the Lord instantly punishes him, and he will rot for thousands of years.

"Look at me, David. I just did something stupid once, I showed the Lord my displeasure and anger, and I've been paying for my mistake for thousands years. The fact is that God demands more from me because I saw Him, and I am the son of the First Man. Accordingly, the punishment is more severe for me than for others. Lucifer was removed away for simply having doubted. When God has brought you closer, you cannot doubt or be afraid; you must unquestioningly serve faithfully and without hesitation accomplish any mission. God creates and God destroys. So, dear David, be truly afraid of the Lord God, you will judge yourself strictly for all the mistakes."

"Thank you for the lesson. I will definitely pray every day."

"Pray, David, pray with all your heart."

Cain collected the money and magnetic cards the administrator had left and handed them to David.

"The guys will eat for this money and you can refuel. Keep the money for yourself, and distribute the cards to everyone."

Together they headed for the exit to the gate and saw the administrator, he stood frozen like a statue and dumbly stared at one point, he could not believe in his memories that Cain had suggested him.

"Dear sir, may I have you for a moment?"

"Sure, how do you like it here?"

"Oh, yes, very good. Please give us one more room."

"Where would you like it?"

"Closer to our suites."

"When do you want to make the payment?"

"Aha, yes, the payment..."

Cain approached the administrator and extended his hand to him, the admin decided to shake hands. Cain squeezed the admin's palm, looked straight into his eyes and said, "We don't owe you anything, we paid everything in cash. Disable the video surveillance and erase all files."

"Certainly, of course. Thank you, we are all very pleased that you have chosen our hotel."

"We appreciate you and we are also very happy."

The administrator, as if in a fog, issued a magnetic card.

"Thanks you."

The admin started rubbing his face. It would be easy to tell to onlookers that the admin took drugs or some kind of pills. He was definitely out of his mind; Cain influenced his mentality and the nervous system. David and Cain went out on the road, the guys stood near the car and smoked.

"You know that if you smoke, God will not take you to Heaven. They smoke only in hell," Cain said aloud and smiled at his own joke.

"Well, brothers, we check in to the hotel and go booze and have fun, Father Nikon treats you all, we have a hell of a heap of money."

 The guys took the cards, collected their belongings and went to check into the hotel rooms.

"You have maximum half an hour to take a shower and change clothes, then we gather near the car."

Cain stood and looked at the sky. What for has God created so many people? Isn't it easier to destroy them all right away? Cai pulled a plastic card out of his pocket and began to examine it. Then he thought, 'Everything is made in China, there are a hell of a lot of these Chinese; they have no thoughts, they are bio robots, people born for permanent work. They don't think about God at all, they don't care, they want to pelt the whole planet with their junk. It is beautifully written in Bhagavad Gita about the division of the humankind into castes. There is something in it. The caste of Chandalas, whom the spiritual does not interest, can work without raising their heads until death. Probably, God had collected and settled in China all Chandalas. In China, they eat dogs, and a Chandala is a synonym of a dog-eater. They will all die and will not even understand why.

Cain thought about taking a shower, but he hated this primitive wash. Cain loved his recreation capsule, designed by the best engineers for him personally. He lied in the capsule, and it did the massage and cleaned his skin with hot silver-purified water, and after all stimulated his body with ultrasound. At the same time, he could watch TV or listen to the music. He raised from the capsule, as if newly reborn. After the capsule, the traditional shower seemed a primitive Stone Age wash. He wanted to find out if they have a *Jacuzzi* or at least a common bath. Cain returned to the hotel, walked straight ahead and at the end of the hallway on the right was his room with a view of the sea. His suitcase and briefcase stood in front of his door. Cain took his things and put them by the bed.

He looked at the sea and remembered some priest; he was stern to all and forced everyone to keep fasting for every trifle sin. At the same time, he liked to partake of delicious food, and in the mornings, he used to treat himself generously to coke. He was such a naughty boy, but he made an important and formidable face, while he himself inside was mocking at everyone. He got addicted to the snow and received the Eucharist at any time; sometimes he even forgot to wipe the powder from the nose. After sniffing a fair dose he used to burn incense, and thurifying the thick smoke around, swung the censer with all his might, while shouting in basso, "Exit thee, Devil, go down, Satan, fall down to hell!"

People watched and earnestly crossed themselves; they loved Father Nikodim. So once Archibald decided to go to him to confession, so we all had great fun. Archibald crossed himself and said, "Forgive me, Father, for I have sinned!"

But the father stands with his back turned on him and sniffs his nose.

"Repent, my son, read twenty times *'Ave Maria'* and also the prayer that I myself composed *'Oh, Jesus, forgive us sinners!'*"

"But shall I pray to God?"

"Pray to God? We are too sinful and too insignificant to address God directly, for this trained people are needed, experienced, as well as saints, they act as mediators. They, our saints, know our sinful souls better!"

"Father, you have your nose white."

"This is flour, my son, we bake cookies here, so I got whitened it with flour."

"Yes, Father, and I would like to receive a blessing from you, what do I need for this?"

"Oh, my son, I must behold your zeal to come to our church not empty-handed, but with the desire to sacrifice and prove to us that everything material is alien to you and that you are ready to live a spiritual life and deny all that is damned material."

"You want me to give you my money?"

"Oh, no, God forbid. If such is your desire, so it is called a donation for the temple."

"But Father, you know, I find myself in strained circumstances. I haven't eaten anything for several days in a row."

"Oh, it's in vain that you torment yourself this way; there is a superb restaurant just around the corner, I advise you."

"But I have no money even to buy bread."

"Aha, it is clear if this is the case, it means that God wants to try you and wants to probe you. The main thing is, you hold out."

"But what if I die of hunger?"

"No, you won't, the main thing is to drink enough water in proper time, so you can last at least forty-five days without food. You won't die right away without food. And during this time you will certainly find something to snatch."

"Are you not afraid of God?"

"Why should I be afraid? Is God to be afraid of? God forgives everything, and we are all sinners. I received my certificate of completion of the seminary. I dedicated all my life to serving the Lord our God Jesus Christ! So I must have some privileges."

"Do you think God is Jesus Christ?"

"Yes, Jesus, the Virgin Mary, the Holy Spirit and God, they all stick together."

"Do you think that Virgin Mary created galaxies?"

"Look, you moron, why you cling to me with your galaxies? Get the fuck out of here, asshole. Galaxies bother him..."

"Okay, why you get so mad, I just asked."

"Why are you snooping around here? Where are you from? I have not seen you before!"

"I am the Reverend Bangingcat!"

All of a sudden, Archibald all lit up from inside and smoothly took off to the air. Father Nikodim collapsed down on his knees and earnestly began to cross himself, but then he thought, 'That's the dust! That's the get off!'"

"Nikodim! Share the powder! You cannot sniff it all by yourself!" Archibald's voice resounded like the rumble of thunder.

"Oh, Your Holiness, I have only a couple of grams left about me, let's fly off together and fetch some more! The powder is cool! Blows your brain! Not diluted, straight from Mexico. Pure like first snow! My treat!"

"On such a beautiful note, Reverend, I'm afraid I should interrupt you. In fact, I am the Devil or Lucifer, as you please, and so I showed up personally for your little filthy soul. In person! God ordered me *personally* to shake your soul out and use it until THEY change their mind there."

Suddenly, the Holy Father's throat became sand dry, and he felt as if a crowbar was stabbed through his chest; heartache made him sick to nausea, and there were ripples in his eyes.

Archibald looked at the Holy Father and did not want his quick death; he wanted to chat with this jolly fellow.

"Wait! No, please give me a chance to repent and amend my misdeeds!"

"God was tired of looking at your disgraces and ordered me to crush you into a squeeze box."

"Wait! Please, don't! I will serve you, I will not use this damned powder anymore!

"You think this all is about the powder? You just recently ditched me to die of hunger, and you feast in a restaurant five times a day!"

"I am a fool, I was stupid, I just made a big mistake!"

"Indeed, you are stupid, Nikodim! I read your thoughts, you're lying to me all the time, you're deceitful and fraudulent! I see you through! What should I do with you? What's your mundane name?"

"Ghhh… Ghhh… May I have some water, please… My name is Denis…"

"Well, Denis, and why did you decide to make for a priest?"

"I evaded the draft, I got a military subpoena and I was very afraid. So I recalled that priests do not go to the army. I went to some parson and clung to him, so he sent me to the theological academy."

"But why did you give God empty vows? Why are you scoffing at believers and mocking them constantly?"

"Because I did not really believe in God, even in our academy no one truly believed. And now, we're just fooling around and making money. There is no crime here and there is always a heap of money. That's not my fault that those fools bring money to us!"

"They are not fools, they are called believers."

"Well, of course, yes, of course, believers… But no one explained anything to me at once, they only said that it was necessary to be strict and then the fools would incur donations and there would be even more money. People carry generous donations when they see a stern and formidable Holy Father; they believe that I can solve all their problems. I coped with it. I shared it with my friends and they granted me a special status and privileges. I do not need to steal or rob, or God forbid, work to buy food or this cursed powder."

"You see, Lucifer is standing before you, and yet you still don't believe in your death and that I will make a thread out of you and throw this thread into the fire so many times, until I invent me something else."

Here, suddenly, Nikodim imagined that this was all happening in his dream. With a great astonishment, he realized that he went over the limit with this insidious powder and lost his senses, and this all was not a reality. The priest jumped up and began to grasp Lucifer with his hands; surprisingly, he was tangible and material. Nikodim thought the dream was very realistic. He began to pinch his hands and rub his ears.

"Now you see me with your own eyes, and I haven't killed you yet; and you still don't believe in my existence. Although any believer would recognize me by smell."

"You are a dream. You are not real."

Nikodim began to feel around him feverishly in hope to find an evidence that he was dreaming about all this.

"See, Nikodim, you sinners, atheists and other comedians, you all are the same. I stand in front of you, and you still deny my existence, and deny death, as a transition to a worse world for you, that will be a world without picnics with girls, without restaurants and without cocaine. I personally guarantee you this for the next several thousand years.

"Get thee behind me, Satan! Go down, Devil!"

Nikodim pulled a censer out of the cabinet and tried to light it, but the lighter would not ignite. Lucifer took the stool and sat down, amusing himself with the sight of the frightened parson, who was clutching at everything and felt around him in search of a weapon against the Devil himself. The he recalled that the interlooper had to be ousted by the Holy Cross. Father Nikodim took off his gold crucifix and began to read the prayer.

"Deliver me, O Lord, from the seduction of the unholy and wicked antichrist near coming, and shelter me from his nets in the hidden desert of Your Salvation! May You grant me, O Lord, the strength and courage of the firm confession of Your Holy Name, and may I not fear and give up of for the sake of the Devil, and will not deny You, My Savior and Redeemer, and from Your Holy Church, but grant me, O Lord,

day and night to cry and shed tears over my sins, and spare me, O Lord, in the hour of Thy Last Judgment. Amen!"

Lucifer looked at the priest with surprised eyes.

"Is that all?"

The Holy Father applied the crucifixion directly to Archibald's forehead head and began to howl another prayer, which he had learned in the seminary, *"Exorcizamus te, omnis immundus spiritus, omnis satanica potestas, omnis incursio infernalis adversarii, omnis legio, omnis congregatio et secta diabolica, in nomine et virtute domini Nostri Jesu!"*

"Listen, *Deniska*, quit this baloney, who invented all this balderdash? Do you really believe I have nothing to do except haunting you? God Himself has sent me to punish you! And you keep on mumbling, 'go down, leave me, get behind'! Then, gold is the metal of sinners, it is my metal, I invented it, so an intelligent person will never put gold on himself. And finally, I thought up the Crucifixion too, nobody executed Jesus, thus there was no Crucifixion. This I developed to take you, people away from God. So what you gonna do now?"

"I really want to wake up."

"You are awake."

"Please, I don't want to die like that!"

"Look, here is a paradox, everyone knows, and knows perfectly well what is good and what is bad. Nevertheless, people always inclined to deceive themselves. The sinner thinks he will live forever, but the righteous is always ready for death, and he accepts death as a transition to a better world, because he knows that he deserved it. However, the sinner knows that he does not deserve anything good and the situation is getting out of his hand. So I ask you in plain words, *Deniska*, do you, fucking moron, realize that the situation is out of your control?"

Denis-*Deniska*, in the spiritual world, Father Nikodim thought that it would not be a sin to whack the uninvited guest on the head. Moreover, as it is Satan himself, then it would count towards his reputation of a righteous servant of God.

Lucifer roared in thundering laughter, "Reverend Father Nikodim, don't make me kill you right away, let's talk a bit more!'

But Denis-Nikodim decided to stand against Lucifer and fight for his life....

Cain was looking at the sea, when there was an abrupt knocking on the door.

"Cai! Open up!"

"Coming!"

Cain stepped forward and opened the front door. Jack appeared in front of him with furious eyes.

"What happened? We've been waiting for you for a whole hour, running around like fools, looking for you everywhere..."

"Oh, I took a nap, reflected on things..."

"Cai, you yourself gave us thirty minutes; are we in a hurry, or not?"

"We are in a hurry. I'll be right there, just wash my face..."

"I'll wait right outside the door; what miracles are happening to you?"

"This is the planet of the dead, Jack, you do not understand. Freedom is when you are not tied to anything and can move at superspeed between galaxies, between different worlds afraid of nothing..."

"It's not in store for me! We are waiting for you, Boss."

Jack closed the door, Cai's face smoothed, and his eyes softened. 'The guys were worried about me. One way, or another, soon we part, no guarantee that THEY will let us remain together.'

Cai opened the tap and waited for the cool water from the faucet to go. Time has flown by like a second; he took icy water in his palms and splashed it on his face. It was high time to advance. He wiped his face and hands, while perceiving every second, the sensations of water on his face and a feeling of cheerfulness. It was as if God sent signals to his head that he would not soon be drinking fresh and clean water again. 'People do not realize the joy of clean water and clean air; they take it for granted and think it must always be so. Oh, no. This is the gift of the Lord!' Cai smiled and said aloud, "Thank you, O Lord, for clean and delicious water!"

Cain left the suite, walked quickly along the hallway and saw a new girl at the reception desk.

"Oh, the administrator has changed!"

"Hello, you checked in at us today and I have to register you into our database. Our administrator did not have time."

"And where is he?"

"He got sick, and left for home."

"I gave him all the data and paid for the rooms!"

"Yes, I don't argue with you, he told me that you paid for all four numbers, but there is no registration, the video recordings are all deleted, I don't even know how to address you."

"My daughter, I am Reverend Father Nikon. I arrived at the monastery with my pilgrim associates."

"Please, find a way to accommodate my request and provide me with your documents."

"Fine."

Cain produced his diplomatic Maltese passport and put it on the reception board.

"I think my passport would be sufficient, the rest of my colleagues may be registered with my last name."

"As a rule, this is not accepted here, but I will make an exception at your request. Tell me, do you remember exactly what sum you have paid?"

"Well, I remember exactly, I gave him a hundred thousand rubles."

"Did he give you the rest?"

"No, I told him to keep the change."

"Oh my God, so what shall I do?"

"So what happened?"

"Wow, it's too bad! I am in a trouble!"

"Tell me, maybe I can help you?"

"I do not have the right to tell it, but everything is lost. The money you paid is lost, and the video is lost. Tell me, have you noticed anything strange? Have you been in the hotel all the time?"

"Yes, the administrator behaved weirdly, now disappeared somewhere, and then suddenly appeared."

"He told me that he was very unwell, and if I had questions, he would be able to answer only tomorrow. He hummed an odd melody, I thought he was either drunk or under the influence. Asked for a time out until tomorrow to sleep off."

"Well then, tomorrow, everything will come to know; and you right away say, 'trouble'! Is it a disaster? The trouble is that what happens to us to inflict detriment irrevocably, that is the trouble! A database, or a camcorder, or money, that's acquirable, that'll come with time."

"You can say whatever you want, but they can dock it off my salary, and for me this is a great problem."

"I don't understand; did I upset you?"

"Forgive me, I was just worried, we haven't had an incident like that yet."

"That's a mere trifle".

Cain went outside and approached the bus; everyone was already seated and waiting for their boss. Only the boss was not in a hurry to get into the car. Cain looked at the sky, inhaled the fresh breeze with a full breast, rubbed his hands very hard and clapped. He concentrated and pondered how to approach Seraphim correctly, so that he would not flee. Then he opened the car door and said, "David, we are going back to the monastery; we will process our good friend Grigori."

"Fine."

Cain sat into the passenger's seat and pondered how to lead the conversation so as not to waste time in vain on unnecessary equivoques. Very quickly, they were near the monastery again. Cain called Lenin, "Volodya, where are you?"

"Here, Master, what you orders will be?"

"Get me that parson."

"He is in church, praying."

"Go stink him there, let him come out to me."

"Fine, I'll get him. Would it be appropriate to interrupt a prayer?"

"The prayer cannot be interrupted if a person earnestly prays to God, and if he only pretends to pray, then you can even kick him in the ass."

"Clear. I'll do everything right away."

Lenin flew up to Hieromonk Grigori and listened to his thoughts and the prayer. Grigori, on his knees, recited memorized prayers automatically, while still reflecting on the pilgrim Nikon, who donated a lot of money. Grigori asked God how to dispose of the funds properly. He asked God to bless this money, if suddenly it were damned money from the Evil. Next to Grigori was a monk Matvey, also deep in a prayer. He prayed, but the unbearable stench prevented him from concentrating. He could not stand it and said aloud, "Where is this stench from? Who of you comes to prayer with unwashed feet? It stinks horrendously!"

Matvey deserved his respect, so no one made a remark to him for frustrating the prayer. Hieromonk Grigori rose, mentally thanked God for everything, and decided to address his brotherhood, "My brethren in Christ, you all know how I love and respect you. I ask you to follow the rules of prayer and not violate them. I ask you to find the source of this foul smell and remove it, wash the floors with caustic and aroma soap pleasant to the Lord; if anyone feels that the smell from him is not fresh, then I ask you to indulge in water procedures. During prayer, nothing should distract us!"

No one said a word. Lenin began to whisper in Hieromonk Grigori's ear, "Go out of the monastery, there is a general unrest! It stinks in the street, and the wind brings this fetid smell to the church!"

The Reverend did not distinguish Lenin's whispering from his thoughts, therefore he turned to the monks, "Therefore, my brethren, Brother Nikon from Russia came to our humble abode today and made a very substantial donation to the temple, so it would be very unpleasant if he now comes to us to the service, and we have such unbearable stench here. Perhaps the stench was blown from the street by wind, so I ask all of you to go out and around the whole monastery."

The monks, silently, began to leave the church and scattered in separate ways. Hieromonk Grigori went straight to the parking lot, where Lenin conducted him in whisper.

"God bless you, my dear brother Grigori! Did you decide to meet me?"

"My dear brother Nikon, I'm glad to see you. What can I do for you?"

"I would like to obtain information about hermit monks who live in the mountains."

"By now, I personally communicate only with Seraphim, he sometimes comes to our temple, and I gladly share with him everything that is necessary."

"And how often does this happen?"

"He goes down when I mentally call him in prayer."

"Remarkable, is that how you communicate?"

"Yes, mentally. You probably find it hard to believe, but after I think of him, two days later he comes to our church."

"Call him; I would like to talk to him!"

"Why, we will get to him faster on foot, he is now in nearby caves."

"Fine, let's go and meet him."

"You go down to the waterfall, and I will change my shoes and catch up with you."

Cain nodded and walked down the road to the waterfall. His retinue followed him. Cain stepped on white stones and thought that these stones had seen many fates. This is a inordinate rarity, usually we walk on asphalt and do not feel the history under our feet. History that reminds us of mistakes and heroic deeds. The museum is not that interesting; everything is rolled up in the asphalt in order to disconnect our bare feet from nature. Consumers' time. Cain took off his shoes and his socks and went barefoot on the rocks. Doesn't God send us signals? Take in your hands a white stone and ask it about the destiny of people who stepped on it. The stone will tell us the whole truth, it will say that it has seen the rain, it has heard the wind, and it has seen human tears and felt shed blood that dropped on it. From this story, any reasonable person will understand that we must improve, become better. We will become better, and perhaps God will forgive us. This white stone surely knows who you were in your past life. Cain in his one life had lived many lives, changed many names, saw many countries and he sees through every person.

Hieromonk Grigori was very afraid of Cain, he could not explain to himself where his instinctive fear of "Father Nikon" had come from. He chased away from himself the thought that Nikon was the Devil incarnate... Then who? His thoughts were confused and he came to the conclusion that Nikon was the Angel of Death whom God had sent to try his decency. Grigori fell in fever; he thought that the money should be well put away, so that no one would be tempted. Hieromonk knew that for this money he would answer with his soul, and he was afraid. He took off his slippers and put on his sneakers. It would be improper to climb the mountains in slippers. Grigori changed his clothes and went to the waterfall at a quick pace. On his way, he thought that he should talk to "Father Nikon" about how to use the assets in the best way so that he would not be covered with shame later. Hieromonk fluttered over to "Father Nikon" and began to tell him the story of New Athos and about the temple. Cain was not interested, but he still silently nodded his head and demonstrated his interest. They climbed the mountain, the places were amazing and Cain admired the beautiful and primordial nature and clean river. A man was walking toward them, and Cain immediately noticed him. Cain yanked and realized that Seraphim himself was going to meet them.

"Look Brother Grigori, a monk is approaching! Do you know him?"

"So, this is… alas, this is our Brother Seraphim!"

"Perfect."

Seraphim went at a calm pace, nevertheless for the first time in many years he felt anxiety in his heart. He looked at the delegation that was going to meet him and thought, 'Am I, O Lord really going to see You soon? Are these people really my death?'

 Seraphim spread his face in a broad smile and went to meet his guests from far away, among them he recognized Gregory. 'I wonder if Gregory knows whom he brought to me. Probably not. God did not bless Gregory with a special insight. Later he would repent.'

When they approached each other on the road at a stone's throw distance, Hieromonk Grigori yelled as if insane, "May God bless you, my Brother Seraphim, I bring pilgrims to you, accept us! They want to see you live and talk to you!"

"Peace to you, my brothers, with my joy! With all my joy and pleasure, my brothers, I will help you!"

They approached each other and Grigori began to hug Seraphim and shake his hand, as if he had not seen him for a hundred years. Seraphim looked Cain in the eye and realized that the Devil got to him. And that he will have a battle to fight, and it will be vitally essential to prove his loyalty to God. Seraphim felt uneasy, he remembered the times of his youth, the feeling was as if after a street fight, he felt dizzy.

"Peace to Thee, Brother Seraphim, I am Brother Nikon, and these are my pilgrim friends, Vassily from Moscow and Jack from America."

"I'm glad to meet you too, for what reason were you looking for me?"

"Well, we didn't exactly look specifically for you, but decided to go about the holy places, talk with the monks, and pray together. And what is very important to me, this is pure faith, faith with all heart and soul, faith without admixtures of empty words and deeds. I am in quest of the Chosen One, in search of the Holy."

"I am not holy."

"No, of course not. But maybe you have some information. I am sure that there is the Chosen One in the mountains."

"You will forgive me, friends, but where did you get such an idea? Who told you that?"

"My Brother Seraphim, in the night prayer, I swore before God that I will always serve faithfully; and on the thirteenth day of dry fasting, a vision appeared to me. As if I were standing in the middle of an eternal swamp, and in front of me there was a column of human bones so tall, that its upper edge was not visible. And I could not move, the swamp sucked me in, and the Voice said, 'If you touch the column, you die!' But I walked to the pillar, and the swamp had been sucking me in, and when only one step left, I was seized by some force which elevated me up higher and higher and this Force said in my ear, 'Do not hurry to die, find the Chosen One and collect the faithful children of Abraham in pairs!' I woke up from this vision of the Lord and set myself the goal, to fulfill the Will of the Lord and do as I was told."

"Father Nikon, how did you recognize that this is the Will of the Lord, and not the Devil? Why should God send you to search for someone?"

"I cannot know this, you're right. But I devoted my whole life to service and had not previously noticed that the Tempter was interested in me. And in the Bible, God also sends dreams and visions. I, that is, we, are the instrument of the Lord. Aren't we?"

"All you say my brother, sounds nice, but my heart is in alarm. In dismay is my heart… Do you not know why?"

"No, I cannot know that."

Seraphim looked Cain in the eye again and felt the danger emanating from him. Hieromonk Grigori walked carelessly and thought about food.

"Brethren, I invite you all to the fratry, they cook deliciously there; we can also partake of homemade wine."

Vassily sensed the tense situation and pretended to play a joker, "Father Nikon, let's snack on something, otherwise I will die of hunger! We are so tired and have not eaten for a long time. I beg you, Holy Father! I will tell you some funny stories, they'll make you laugh."

"Okay, my son, if you got hungry, let's enjoy the local cuisine."

Seraphim did not like all this, and he did not wish to go along with them.

"You forgive me, but I'd rather refuse. I keep a strict fasting, and I will not be able to share the enjoyment of a meal with you. It's my prayer time."

"I get it, fine. See, the matter is that I have a message for you."

Cain extended his both hands towards Seraphim. Seraphim realized that he could not leave that easy; he reluctantly stretched out his hands to Cain. When their hands touched, Seraphim saw the Earth on fire, and whole mountains of the dead bodies... and through the fire, he heard a profound voice, speaking to him, "Come with us, My Brother Seraphim, you can change everything."

Seraphim came to his senses, and realized that his life was over and that the trial began.

"My brother Seraphim, the choice is yours. You can get to Paradise alone or..."

"Or you will kill millions for me alone?"

"Yes."

"What do you want from me?"

"Now we eat and drink wine, taste some barbecue, and ponder over for a while together."

Cain took Seraphim under his arm and dragged him aside. Hieromonk Grigori was shocked by an incomprehensible conversation; he could not understand what was going on. He never saw fear in the voice and in the eyes of Seraphim. He was at a loss.

Vassily embraced Grigori and said, "So what will we eat?"

"I don't understand what they are talking about..."

"Oh, that's about the past. Seraphim is Seraphim for you, and through our databases he passes as Leonid Fitozov, a Pontian who escaped from Greece. He's been wanted for a long time, and now he is hiding in these blessed mountains and pretending to be a holy man."

"Are you from the police?"

"Well, yes and no. Our structure is a different *kontora*. Vassily pulled out a certificate from the Ministry of Defense and shoved it under the nose of the horrified Hieromonk."

"Why did you lie to me all the time?"

"Because you would not turn in your hermit."

"Will you arrest him?"

"No, but he would be obliged to co-operate, otherwise we will take measures and extradite him over to the Greek authorities. Behind him, there are more than twenty bank robberies and many armed assaults. He is an extremely dangerous gangster who had also created an entire criminal syndicate."

"I did not know, but you see, he repented. He is no longer a gangster and has nothing to do with these matters anymore."

Cain embraced Seraphim's shoulder and headed towards the dining room.

"Seraphim, Seraphim, Seraphim, a beautiful name, so why did you choose such a name for yourself? Do you even know what that means? Formerly, the six-winged angels were called Seraphs or Seraphims, those were pillars of fire. God sent the Seraphims for requital. And you called yourself Seraphim… why?"

"Because I wanted so."

"But you are Leonid Fitozov. Why didn't you keep the name Leonid? Leonid, Leonidas, descendant of a lion! A beautiful Greek name. And now you took the burden on you, calling yourself Seraphim."

"What do you want?"

"I want to understand, why you, Lyonia, a thug and a murderer, stepped so swiftly on the path of correction? And how did it happen that you were heard, while others were heard less?"

"Who are you?"

"I am Cain, you know who I am?"

"The one from the Bible? Son of Adam? The father of all killers?"

"Do not insult me, I did not kill a single person for money, but you did. So the question is: why do THEY hear you, but not me?"

"It's very simple, it's because you still have where to fall, and there's already an abyss beneath me. Your soul will never be as punished as mine will; therefore, my efforts are evaluated differently. Secondly, my dear forefather, I do not ask God for forgiveness or life in paradise, since my actions are not subject to forgiveness. I punish myself, and I do not want to go to Heaven to God, knowing that I am a worthless nothing, and you are Cain, striving to go to Heaven, because you consider yourself worthy and the best! So this is your mistake. Your mistake is that you consider yourself the best! Your friend Lucifer made the same mistake; he also still considers himself the most intelligent and the best. And you know that THEY really do not like it. I, am Seraphim, I am ready to die, to suffer and die again, I am no longer Leonid, I am not like a lion, I am a fiery pillar. I myself suffer, my soul is already burning from my sins and I cannot turn back time."

"You talk a lot. I need you to go with me to Germany for the research."

"What kind of research?'

"The idea is to take your DNA and check its reaction to various diseases. German scientists suggest that a serum can be created from the blood of a believer to cure cancer and other deadly diseases."

"It is clear, that means that God sends some souls a trial by diseases, and we will heal them?

"Listen, you can talk this way about anything."

"I see. And if I do not go, will you burn the city after the city in turn?"

"Yes. You know the truth and you know that I am not bluffing."

"Fine. And the papers?"

"Vasya will get ready everything perfectly."

"So as it is, I'm ready."

Cain was very happy; he tried not to show his joy that he played the bullet chess so successfully and achieved his goal. At the meantime, Seraphim mentally prayed God for events to unfold according to the Will of the Lord. Seraphim raised his head and said, "My brethren in Christ, before partaking of this meal, I ask you to allow me to take a wash and indulge in prayer."

Cain looked at Seraphim and sensed a trick. Cain wondered if Seraphim would run away from him.

"I will not run away from you, do not be afraid, I will pray before your eyes."

Seraphim went behind the fratry, chose a place away from the road and knelt.

"O Creator, save me, protect me from the Evil, I am your humble slave Seraphim. Shelter me from this person, for he started a blasphemy!"

Cain realized that the Seraphim was asking God for intercession and immediately called Vladimir Lenin. The lost soul appeared, and again the stank of old rags and dirty feet announced him, "I listen to you My Master."

"Be near him, bother him, and listen to what he says."

"Fine."

Seraphim felt the heat and realized that his prayers were heard. Seraphim decided to continue to pray, but a sharp stench of *The Roquefort Cheese* distracted him from the prayer. Then unnecessary thoughts invaded his mind; did he step onto someone's excrement? Moreover, God forbid he kneeled down on it, and there was no water… Seraphim began to look around. He got up from his knees and began to examine his place of prayer.

Cain called him loudly, "Seraphim, my brother, we have to go, let's join our brethren!"

Seraphim went in the direction of Cain's voice. They walked into the fratry together. Cain approached David, who always walked in the tail, not listening to the conversations and not delving into them.

"Come on, David, get the bus, we'll go back to the hotel, and if we can, we'll go to Sochi today. We do not need any delay."

"You got it. Now I'll drive to the entrance."

Cain wanted to leave Abkhazia as quickly as possible while Seraphim was in his hands and did not change his mind.

"I think it's time for me to eat well, Grigori, my brother, let's drink some wine for good farewell."

Hieromonk Grigori was in a strong blow, involuntary tears flew down his cheeks, for he betrayed the holy man. He felt himself a Judas. Gregory fought in his youth and he was not a cowardly man, so he decided to act.

He knew that all things had to be done on time, because later prayer would not save,

and then he would devour himself from inside. Hieromonk knew that the guys were all in good physical shape and he could not cope with them with bare fists, he needed a gun or machine gun. Hieromonk called his neighbor and childhood friend and in the Abkhaz language quickly and lispingly chatted, "I'm in trouble, call my aunt *Tiotia Tamara* and Grandpa. I'm in our fratry."

"I'm on my way, Brother!"

Hieromonk with a smile took cranberry compot and drank it to the bottom, mentally imagining himself a glass of vodka, he remembered the war, and his body caught fire, and tears again appeared in his eyes, 'Okay, dick suckers, you won't get Seraphim, I'll give my life for him, but he will not leave.'

Grigori mentally heated himself. Cain did not pay attention to the priesthood, he did not take his eyes off Seraphim and watched him chewing cabbage salad and sipping homemade wine in small sips…

Suddenly two highlanders broke into the fratry; one of them released a short squirt from a *Kalashnikov.*

"Mugs down on the floor! Now!"

Hieromonk smiled wickedly and said, "So you came to me like that, you pulled me out of prayer, slipped bloody smelly money on me, and then set me up as a kid and made me a traitor?"

Jack jumped up in an attempt to grasp the machine gun. Several shots in rapid succession reverberated under the high ceiling of the fratry, and Jack dropped dead.

"I would not advise you to set your own terms here."

Cain looked at the dead Jack with his eyes open and his heart sank, 'Again, I lost a friend! What a twist!'

"Listen Grigori, calm down. What do you want?"

"I do not need anything, Seraphim is not going anywhere!"

Grigori turned to his friend and said, "Brother, give me a gun."

One of the assaulters handed the Hieromonk Grigori a 7.62 TT, *Tulski Tokarev*, they called this gun *Tiotia Tamara,* "Aunt Tamara." Automatic assault rifle 7.62 AKM *Kalashnikov* in their argot was called *Dedushka*, "Grandpa".

He walked over to Vassily lying on the floor, and kicked him.

"You, asshole, look at me! Have you come to my country to oppress people? Give me your card, I'll read. Vassily pulled out his ID and handed it to Gregory.

"So, Vassily, major... and where is that other ID that you used to scare me?"

"So this is it."

"No, there was the Ministry of Defense, I did not finish reading. But in principle, I do not fucking care. Farewell Vassily, see you in hell!"

Hieromonk pulled the trigger and drove four bullets into Vassily. The torn body of Jack lay on the floor. Seraphim was silent, he decided not to interfere and lay on the floor and did not move. He thought, "God saves in His way." Cain was very upset and stood on his straight legs and immediately got shot in the stomach from the TT. It was very painful.

"You, whatever-you-call-yourself, Father Nikon, or anything else! I don't care about you, I will not kill you, I will leave you to the will of the Lord; if you survive, get the hell out of here for good, and make so, that I will not see you again. Next time I see you, I'll shoot you in the head and saw your body into pieces and burn them, then you will be difficult to collect."

Cain could not get up; the bullet damaged his insides. Cain tore off his cross and threw it at Grigori.

"ARCHIBALD! Save me!"

Grigori addressed Seraphim, "My brother, forgive me, I have made a great sin against you, God will not forgive. They deceived me; I could not betray you. My Brothers will lead you to the mountains; there this bastard can no longer reach you. Go with my brothers, quickly!"

Hieromonk got down on one knee and with all his might pounded Cain on the head with the butt of the gun. Cain lost consciousness...

'What should a person go through in order to achieve his goal? What should a person sacrifice? Life, health, love, friendship, loved ones?' Cain wanted to die more than ever, nothing kept him on this sinful Earth anymore. Friends whom he loved left him.

Archibald ascended from his chair and raised his two hands up. Two shadows appeared nearby.

"Kill everyone except Seraphim. Confine their dirty souls in capsules and send to me. Help Cain. Get on with it!"

 At that time, Cain was lying on the floor already in his mind and mentally trying to summon David. David heard shots and came running by himself, he saw everything, but was very afraid, he knew that he would also be killed inevitably, if he showed up. David waited for everyone to leave and immediately ran to Cain.

"Father Nikon, what should I do?"

"Help me get up and get to the car. We need to get out of here before the police arrive."

David tried to give support to Cain, but Cain was too heavy. David quickly wondered how to get out of the situation and saw the cook, who was hiding in the kitchen .

"Hey you, come up here, help me!" But the woman could not move.

David approached the cook and raised her to her feet. The cook was shocked by the occurrence; fear froze her horse-like body.

"Can you hear me? Help me, Holy Father, the priest is dying, we need to take him to the hospital now, I alone cannot carry him."

The cook, who was twice as wide as David, and ten times stronger, woke up and asked, "What has happened? How it all began? Monks and priests started the war?"

"Yes, they are fighting over the parish."

The powerful she-cook grabbed Cain's arm and hopped him on her shoulder. The female was bulky and mighty like a hippo. David supported Cain on the other side. So they rather quickly got to the car, David opened the sliding door and they laid Cain on the back seat. Cain silently gritted his teeth.

The demons appeared very quickly and began treating Cain, the bullet fell out and the internal organs healed in seconds.

"Urmas and Radokan! Well done. Catch up Seraphim! Stop him."

Seraphim, together with Hieromonk's friends, were rushing along the winding mountain road towards the Georgian border, when suddenly the right front wheel of their car tore off while on the move, the car turned over and hit against a concrete block. Grigori's friends, who sat in front, died instantaneously. It was a sudden death. Seraphim lay stunned upside down in the car. He was squeezed between the front and back seats, and could not get out of the wrecked car.

Cain already knew the place of the accident and raced with David to save Seraphim. Immediately, many people gathered at the scene of the accident and they wanted to pull out Seraphim, this would not work, because the car was crushed and his legs were clamped. They had to either cut or unclench the passenger compartment. Seraphim was waiting for Cain. David, breaking all the rules of the traffic, was in a hurry to the scene of the accident.

Meanwhile, Grigori ascended to his cell, approached the images of the saints who were hanging above the bed, and knelt down.

"O Lord Almighty, forgive me my sins."

A dark shadow swept before the icons. The Hieromonk could not say anything more, his heart stopped abruptly, and he fell dead with his eyes and his mouth wide open.

Demons returned to Archibald with three small crystal balls.

"Aha, these are the brave guys who tried to confuse my plans."

He put one ball in his palm and as if weighing it.

"This soul is pure, honest, and courageous. You had still fifteen years on the Earth. I will install you into the body of the newborn son of one of the most influential drug barons in Latin America. Live in wealth and luxury, maybe you will commence to sin and continue your tenure on the Earth."

Archibald crushed the capsule and the soul flew away. There were still two capsules left. He took the next capsule.

"Hieromonk Grigori, that's the meeting! You tried. Your time is thru. THEY require you. You did it. You earned your eternal life, congratulations."

He crushed Gregory's capsule and sent his soul to God. Then Archibald took the last capsule and smiled. There was a sinful soul inside and its stay was supposed to be very long.

"Still two hundred and ten years of imprisonment here on the Earth; you will be born in the family of your neighbor Beslan, with whom your family is hostile. You will fight against your own kin. Or even vice versa, your children will fight against you."

Archibald crushed the last capsule and so ordered the souls. Only Hieromonk Grigori was lucky. He went to God, and in the monastery, he would be considered holy, because he died during the prayer. The monks were also delighted that before his death, he obtained the money to repair the monastery and thus fulfilled his mission on the Earth.

To the brave and faithful, God bestows reason in life and paradise after death.

Hieromonk was cleared and went on. He will not return to the Earth again.

David could not drive further, a traffic jam formed, and David drove into the oncoming lane. A traffic inspector jumped out and blocked their way. David stopped, the inspector approached the driver's window, "Hello, please present your documents. You violated the traffic rules and created an emergency situation."

Cain got out of the van, it was still painful for him to move, but he gathered his strength, approached the inspector and took him by the hand. The inspector wanted to jerk away his hand from Cain's grip, but in a split second, he looked into Cain's eye and yielded. The inspector's consciousness failed, and he could barely stand on his feet, like a drunk. Cain whispered in his ear, "We are from the Ministry of Internal

Affairs of Abkhazia, you are obliged to obey me and fully assist in everything. Are we clear?"

"Exactly so, we are clear," the officer obediently saluted.

"It's a simple matter, there our suspect got into an accident, he should be carefully pulled out of the wrecked car and put in our car."

"Exactly so."

"We will drive as close as possible, and you will go with us."

"Exactly so."

Cain got back into the minivan, the inspector stood near the door, "Where should I sit? Where is my seat?"

"Sit down in front."

The inspector sat in the passenger's seat, and David continued to move along the contraflow lane. David pulled over to the shoulder to allow ambulance and firefighters to travel. Cain got out and headed straight for the turned over car, there was already a crowd of people and everyone was debating how to pull out the unlucky guy who was stuck there. Two corpses lay on the shoulder near the car, Seraphim hung upside down in an inverted state. Cain went straight to the car and Seraphim saw him.

"You always get what you need, yeah?"

"I cannot order you, you must decide it voluntarily. So far, you failed to get away from me and still you are unlikely to leave. The reason is that you do not understand the structure of the world."

"I'll go with you, and you don't have to kill people."

"The death of a person is not the worst thing that can happen to him. The problem is that your importance falls down with the death of every next person."

Cain mentally called the demon, 'Urmas! Unbend the iron gently.' The metal became soft like a cloth; Seraphim freed himself and fell on his head.

Any matter has its own key, and demons know the key to any matter on the Earth. With the knowledge of this key, and this is a sound or a Word, which is not heard to an ordinary person, it is possible to change the properties of any matter and move it through the air. Pyramids were built this way. They knew the Word or had a demon under their command who knew this Word.

Seraphim got out of the broken into the trash car; his face was smeared with blood. Cain mentally addressed the demon:

'Radokan, check the injuries and health of Seraphim.'

Cain looked at Seraphim and said, "Three scratches and four bad bruises. It is a playgame! Will heal in no time. Seraphim, are you coming with us or will you get there yourself?"

"I'm going with you. I will not run away."

"David, we are going back to the hotel, we take a break there and think about how to proceed."

Cain wanted to wash his face, and sit in silence. Seraphim interested him less and less. Cain was very angry. He wanted to smear Seraphim against the wall. He had no desire to mess with him and beat around the bush. Because of this Seraphim Cain lost his closest people, with whom he had fun and comfort. Cain lost his sense of humor. David was silent, he did not expect such a development of events, but he decided for himself to go with Cain to the end. Cain silently got out of the car and went straight to his room, without talking to anyone. Seraphim addressed David, "I don't understand, what should I do?"

"There are two rooms in the hotel at your choice, take yourself any of them and wait. We will wait until Father Nikon calls us."

"Clear."

David took his bag and quickly went to the hotel, to his room, which Cain had arranged for him. Seraphim went into the hotel, there were no people in the lobby, it was empty. He did not know where to get the keys to the rooms; he sat on the sofa and fell asleep. The dream was very real, he dreamed of a bank robbery in Athens. In this dream, he was a robber and shot from a double barreled shotgun at the bank employee, but he did not fall down, he simply waggled his index finger at him and said,

"If you don't want to be the Chosen One, then be like everyone else and swim with the flow. The Devil is interested only in those who swim against the current."

"Mister, Mister, wake up! Who are you?"

"Ah, aah, I am Leonid Fitozov, please give me the keys to two numbers that have already been paid for by father Nikon."

"Are you a pilgrim too?"

"Yes, I am a pilgrim too, I travel with them and I will decide which room I will stay in; are they double rooms?"

The administrator did not exactly like Father Nikon and his pilgrims; it seemed to her that they brought bad luck to the hotel. Therefore, she did not want to dispute with them.

"Yes, there are two numbers, take the keys, then leave them here."

Seraphim took the keys and walked down the hall, looking at the numbers on the doors. Number seven. 'This is my number,' Seraphim thought.

Cain warmed himself under a hot shower. He tried to collect his thoughts and spirit intact. He had a mess in his head, his thoughts were confused, this situation knocked him off balance. Anger prevented him from thinking reasonably, drums were beating in his temples and his hands were burning. He had a strong inclination to kill, to kill Seraphim without judgement and trial. He stood under the shower in his underwear and socks, his hand automatically switched the lever from hot water to ice cold. He tried to recover. A shadow appeared nearby.

"Urmas and Radokan. What the hell do you want?"

The voice sounded inside his head, 'We came to stabilize you. Do not worry; we will now remove unnecessary pathogens, and we will soothe and calm you down.'

"Don't poke around inside me!"

'It is necessary, Archibald ordered to calm you down.'

In a minute, Cain felt as if slightly intoxicated. Those invisible creatures are able to regulate the internal state of any person. Therefore, many scientists and psychologists cannot explain some mental diseases. For example, a person lives calmly and evenly, but then, all of a sudden, kills his entire family and ends up in suicide.

The church imposes on the believers that the prayer of the priest is able to exorcise a demon. But the demon just does not intervene in man by his will, independently, the Devil orders the demon, and God allows this action. Then, perhaps, God will be able to forgive and recall the demon, but this rarely happens. An ordinary person, whoever he may be, even a priest, cannot influence the demon.

Cain felt great. He undressed completely and enjoyed the hot shower; the burden in his chest was gone. After a shower, he decided to lie down for a while and enjoy the view of the sea. Clarity of mind returned to him.

"Urmas, Radokan. Where are my friends now, Vassily and Jack?"

'Their fate is unknown to us, THEY summoned them immediately to THEMSELVES, and they are not here on the Earth.'

Cain thought that God could forgive them, they earnestly believed in God, and did not sin more than the others. 'Well, without them it will be harder for me.' Cain marveled directly from the bed at the sight of the calm Black Sea. Time had passed, it was already getting dark, and Cain looked at the sea in a good mood. Peace and quiet.

Suddenly, with the strong stench of dirty rags Vladimir Lenin appeared, 'Archibald asks you, do you need help or you will cope yourself?'

"Why should I worry about getting out? Seraphim agreed to go with me. Now let him order his demons, and they will take us anywhere. Right?"

'If Archibald orders, they will deliver you anywhere.'

"Well, now I will have a cup of tea, talk to my friend and we will fly home, without airports and without borders, with the aid of Urmas and Radokan. So pass my word to him."

"You got it."

Cain went out into the hall and walked over to the reception desk; the girl saw Father Nikon and reluctantly headed for him.

"Good evening. What can I do for you?"

"My child, make me, please, some delicious tea."

"We have no option of serving coffee or tea. You should go to the cafe across the road and they will make for you whatever you want."

"If you don't make me coffee now, I'll turn you into a toad. You are stupid, arrogant and boorish woman, starting to get pretty annoying to me."

"I'm calling security now and they will calm you down."

Cain decided not to engage in a quarrel with the stupid woman and said nothing. David heard the conversation in the lobby and quickly jumped out of his room, "Father Nikon, where are we going? What should I do?"

"Here, my son, I wanted to see you and talk. You know who I am?"

"Yes, you are Cain, the son of Adam and Eve from the Bible."

"Right. That's my boy. So, thank you for your help, you done well. Use the money, as we agreed. Perhaps soon troubles are nearing the whole human race, so pray. Only prayer will save you from troubles. Remember my words. Now, get ready and drive home to your family."

"Thank you very much, I will remember you."

"Nothing to thank me for, I draw closer to God with every good deed. Thus I do well to myself."

"Still, I appreciate you."

"Come on, drive out of here, get lost!"

Cain smiled and patted David on the shoulder and headed without glancing back to Seraphim's room. Cain knocked on the door; the door was open."

"Seraphim, are you here?"

"Yes."

Seraphim's voice sounded strange, Cain entered the room and saw a hermit who was lying on the floor in his underpants, drunk off his ass.

"What a fucking piece of shit you are, why so many problems with you? The demons will not drag drunk; you knew that, or are you just a stupid animal?"

"No, I'm not an animal, I'm just like everyone else. Do you know how long I have wanted to get drunk, to smoke and feel an ordinary man again?'

"You are the Chosen One! You are not an ordinary man! You cannot shoot the fucking vodka and smokes, while obscuring your sanity and killing your willpower given to you by the Almighty!"

"I never sought this; I simply felt the need for solitude and prayer."

"Clear, God wants to show us how THEY can make a perfect diamond out of ordinary clay."

"I will take two aspirins, stand in a cold shower, and I will become like a fresh cucumber again."

"Demons can't tolerate the hangover odor; they won't carry you. For them, the smell of alcohol is an unbearable stench. Did you know that?"

"Where from? Did I communicate with demons? I do not believe in hellish devilry."

"This is not devilry, it is the working team of the Creator of Worlds and we do not like the smell of hangover."

"I'm going to the bathhouse now; I'll take aspirin, swim in the sea and recover quickly. Don't get mad, I'm just an ordinary man, but not what you want me to be. I have long wanted to shoot some booze, I simply had no money."

"You cannot do it, and don't even try".

"What exactly?"

"Pretend to be a common tough guy-*mouzhik*. I know who you are, so nobody needs this circus. I also forgot to warn you that I read thoughts, and I read this phrase in your head, *'The devil needs only those who swim against the current, be like everyone else, and the devil will not be interested in you!'*

"Read in my head?"

"Yes. Chill down. Nobody pushes you, if you don't want to fly with me, as you wish, go wherever you want, I'm not keeping you here anymore."

"What's changed?"

"I don't know, I lost my friends and lost interest in you."

"It's not me who killed them!"

"You killed them! You prayed, and God switched on the monk. Your prayer killed my friends, and crippled me, and if it were not for Archibald, I would have suffered with such a wound for at least another six months. You know the power of the Word; the Word is stronger than any weapon!"

"You're right. I asked God that THEY would stop you. Perhaps God has already stopped you, since you have lost interest in me."

"Stopped. All the same, paradise is not in store for you, there will be no discounts. God did not forget your malicious deeds."

"But who told you that I want to Paradise? I evaluated my misdeeds and decided to work off all sins, and this is at least four lives. I want to learn how to transfer knowledge from one life to another in order not to waste time."

"That won't be allowed to you. This is called a trick."

"This is what God decides. If THEY allow, then I can redeem my sins much faster, go through any trials and be cleansed."

"I know for sure that Archibald can trace, after death, where the soul would fly. Then, when you grow up in a new body, Archibald can tell you about your past life and tell you what your tasks are. You know that everything happens by the Will of the Lord God and our meeting is not an accident."

"Is that a deal you are proposing to me now?"

"No, just telling you about our capabilities."

"You know, I don't need anything from the Devil, even if he grants me power over all people and superpowers after death, I won't accept it. I won't take anything from the Devil."

"The Devil is another part of God! God created the Devil and THEY rule all, and the Devil too. And I'm right, aren't I?"

"You're right. Only I do not need anything. See, I asked God to leave you behind me, and your friends died. I would not want to harm anyone anymore. I want to live my life in peace and die."

"I will ask you just one question. Does God know about you?"

"Yes."

"Then why does he allow our communication?"

"God is checking on me."

"But why don't you run away?"

"I myself am interested. Tell me, what you want to do?"

"I want to prove that a person's DNA alters at the moment when the person begins to believe in God and starts to pray. I wanted to prove that, for example, your blood is different in composition from that of a common person. Why do you think it is written in the Qur'an that in a battle one faithful believer in Allah equals to fifty armed and trained soldiers? Because DNA and blood are different, they are absolutely other beings, the Chosen Ones. The color of the energy field of the Chosen changes, and all holy and unholy beings, angels and spirits, and others, they all see this mark and, accordingly, treat him with great care. I call them "the children of Abraham", there are very few of them, and you are the brightest among them".

"Very interesting. So, what is next? What is your goal?"

"My goal is obvious; it is to create a virus that will kill everyone except the Chosen. We will clean the planet from filth."

"So you are going to decide that instead of God?"

"I think that if God did not want this, we would not have ever met. If God does not intervene in events, then God agrees."

"Now, what about the potential future of each person? I used to be a simple guy, I did a lot of bad things, but then, after many years, I came to believe in God. Thus, this virus would have killed me in my youth; but now this virus will pass me by, right? So how many sinners are there like me, who after years grow wiser and find God? But you don't give them that chance."

"You are right, this is called projection. It must be a very long time to wait. This process needs to be accelerated. A virus kills in twenty-one days, and if a person starts praying right away, on the first day, then he will be saved. God will give everyone a chance for salvation and the right to leave this world faster and with a pure soul."

"In other words, you want to make everyone pray to God?"

"Yes, if they pray to God, the Creator of Worlds, for twenty one days in a row, their DNA will change and they will survive."

"Do you think it is reasonable to actually force everyone to pray before the fear of death?"

"Are you, Seraphim, afraid of God?"

"Yes, I am very afraid of God."

"So you do not believe the way everyone else does. You do not think God is an old grandfather with a bad memory, who forgives everything and everyone. Why are you afraid? Nobody is afraid, except for you, and me; the rest are not afraid. So, let's teach them to be afraid too. People are not afraid of God, so they lie, cheat, rob, steal and kill. If they believed in God and were afraid of the wrath of THEM, then the planet Earth would live differently and my friend Archibald would be out of work."

"You telling the truth. But can this be the idea of God, so that people with their mind come to God voluntarily and begin to fear and respect THEM?"

"Bullshit. How many smart people are on the planet, and they consider themselves pundits; they teach in universities but never come to God in their minds. And thus, as soon as someone has a bad incurable cancer or some other non-treatable sore, they dump their books and start praying. Why does a person only under the threat of death begin to believe in God and turns off his rational mind?"

"Sheer truth. I also came to God through utter pain. I have been being tightly on junk and shot myself a triple dose. They pumped me out in the hospital, and after that, I changed."

"Now I'll pour you some water, spell over it, and you drink it. You'll sober up. It's time for us to fly."

Cain poured a full glass of water and spoke the words above the water. Water is like a memory drive in the literal sense. Water can be programmed for any need. Water absorbs prayers and heals the body and soul. Also, if cursing language is used, then it brings death to the one who drinks.

Cain recited over the water and handed it to Seraphim. Seraphim took the glass and drank it down to the bottom.

"That's so, Seraphim. Are you ready?"

"Yes. I feel great!"

Cain summoned Lenin.

"I listen obediently, Master."

"Ask Archibald for the names of the demons so that I can drive them."

"They are already waiting for your command."

"Perfect."

Cain pondered how to do better and where to go. He had to contact *Bayer*, namely, his newly-qualified partner, Robert Baumann.

"Lenin!"

"Yes, Master!"

"How can I get in touch with this jerk Robert Baumann from *Bayer*?"

"He's at the main office; the number is, Germany 0214300."

"Okay. I'll call this moron now and see how much he has advanced. I'll be back soon."

Cain went out into the hall and saw the administrator; the girl was pretending not to notice him.

"Girlie, *devushka*! It's me, listen to me please!"

"Yes, I am listening to you," the admin said reluctantly.

"I really need a call to Germany."

Cain took the administrator's hand and she tumbled through the looking glass, her will completely obeyed him.

"Give me all your money and your documents."

"Okay."

The administrator, totally mesmerized, started to collect money and pulled out her documents and wallet. She gathered everything and put it on the registration desk.

"Here. This is all the money I have and my documents."

Cain grabbed the money, shoved it in his side pocket, held the documents in his hand and continued to suggest, "I have just found your passport and I return it to you, but the money was stolen from you. Two shiny men came down from the sky and took your money. Remember. Erase all records from the video recorder. Pour water on the monitors, keyboards and all the equipment!"

"Okay."

The administrator went to destroy the video recorder. Cain took the phone and dialed Germany.

"Hello, *Bayer Company* welcomes you. What can I do for you? My name is Helga Schmidt."

"This is Cai von der Linde, and I urgently need *Herr* Robert Baumann."

"Now I will contact him at once, wait a second, please."

"Baumann here, I'm listening to you."

"This is Cai, do you remember me? How is our contract? Is the lab ready?"

"Hello, Mr. Cai, nice to hear you! Initially, we will be able to use our main laboratory for DNA research, and then, by the time the research is over, we will get our laboratory ready for the development and production of the agent."

"Fine, where is it better to meet?"

"Here, in Leverkusen, if you don't mind. I'll be waiting for you."

"Fine. Till tomorrow."

Cain thought that there was no point in rushing and he had time until tomorrow. He did not want to stay in Abkhazia, this country left a bitter aftertaste caused by the loss of close friends. He walked through the hall to his room, packed his things; it was one suitcase and a briefcase.

"Urmas! Please, at the behest of Archibald, transfer my belongings to Archibald's *Zur Meise*."

 Suitcase and briefcase disappeared from his sight.

"This is a real trick. This is a mystery to any physicist! "Cain thought.

He went to his bathroom and washed his face. 'What a delicious and healing water is here!' Cain thought. He wiped his face and hands, walked out of his suite and headed towards the Seraphim's room. The administrator walked past him totally at a loss.

'This will serve them a courtesy lesson!' Cain smiled inside.

He didn't need this money; for him it was just pieces of paper, but he knew that for most people, these colored papers were the meaning of life. Therefore, he manipulated people with money.

"Seraphim! Are you ready? Are there any things of yours?"

"I have no things, I am ready."

"Urmas! At the behest of Archibald, transfer Seraphim straight into the hall of Archibald's *Zur Meise*."

Seraphim disappeared.

'This is the trick no one can repeat,' Cain thought again and smiled.

"Radokan! Transfer me by the behest of Archibald to *Zur Meise*."

Cain left blessed Abkhazia and returned to his familiar world, to Switzerland.

DNA

Archibald sat by the fireplace and reflected on his prospects. He was thinking about how much time he had to wait. Archibald wanted back to God. He wanted to return everything as it was before, he wanted to become the First Archangel again, and now distant he is from the house of the Lord for many thousands of sun years. He was sent to exile here on the Earth, where every day dust falls and matter permanently disintegrates. The idea of a virus may change attitude towards God, Archibald will create the conditions to weed out the wicked and leave only the righteous people.

Those will be the Chosen Ones, they will all pray devotedly and earnestly, and then God will be delighted with his creatures and Lucifer will prove that he is right, that people have the right to life, for they are devoted to God. Human souls will not remain for thousands of years on the Earth, but will live here only one life. There will be Paradise on the Earth; all evil spirits will die out, only the Chosen Ones will remain. Suddenly Archibald felt for a split second a cold breeze, sitting in a chair. A suitcase and a briefcase appeared in front of him.

"Aha, my son finished the job and came home! Well, hello, my beloved friend." There was no one in the room; Archibald looked at the suitcase and knew that his friend Cain would appear any next minute.

Suddenly, instead of Cain, Seraphim appeared in his worn black cassock.

"Wow! So who are you? A monk?"

"I am Seraphim, and who are you?"

"Seraphs are six-winged angels, and you are a common fellow, so tell me, what is your name? What name did your parents give you?"

"Leonid."

"There you are. So, you yourself chose the name Seraphim. Right?"

"That is very much so indeed."

"Fine. My name is Archibald. Nice to meet you."

"Aha. You mean you are the Devil in flesh?"

"Yes. People call me that, and imagine me as a horny guy on goats' hoofs, although I have no relationship with an artiodactyls. Dia means God, and a goat is a hoofed creature. Do I look goat type? Ha-ha-ha. No, people are stupid, and you Seraphim is not a stupid man, so do not call me by this ridiculous nickname. God is the Creator; God created me and created all of you. I am an angel, once the brightest angel, the Creator sent me to the Earth and I manage every affair on the Earth. My cherished dream is to return to God, so I want to come to terms with THEM, to find a common denominator. I want to finish my service on the Earth and you will help me in this."

"But does Our Lord God agree with your plan?"

"I listen every day, nevertheless, for now THEY are silent. If the Creator does not like my idea, I would know; then I will immediately stop everything."

A swift breeze blew and Cain appeared.

"Well, hello. I see that you have already got acquainted."

"Yes. Seraphim is an interesting fellow. He probably thought that I have horns and stink of sulfur."

"No, concerning the horns, I definitely didn't expect you wear them; but I thought you were uglier and horrifying. However, you look like a prosperous young man. It's very unusual for me."

"People are accustomed to classify everyone by appearance. It is written on every fence; in every book, it is written that appearance is deceptive, and you still evaluate a person by his appearance. This is how you constantly burn your fingers, but still do not grow wiser."

"No, I know enough about you, and what I read about you is more than enough for me. I do not need evidence; I know your capabilities."

"Fine, Seraphim, it is easy for me to communicate with enlightened people. Do you know what I want from you?"

"Yes, examine my DNA."

"Right. You settle down, if you want, stay here, and if you are not comfortable in my premises, then Cai will check you in a hotel."

"I'll stay here, if you please."

Archibald turned and headed for the door.

"Shall we? I'll show you your guest room."

Cain silently looked into the fire and did not move.

Seraphim went after Archibald. This house was modestly furnished, without superfluous luxury and without much pomp. Everything was very temperate. Archibald opened the door and entered the room; Seraphim followed him. The room had a bed and a TV; the window looked onto the street. There was another glass door in the room.

Archibald, without turning around, said, "Here is our humble lair, your bed, there is a large bathroom behind the glass door, you need to change your clothes. Here is the wardrobe, in the closet all the clothes and shoes are of your size. I advise you to take a bath and get a good sleep; we have a lot of work ahead in the morning."

Archibald turned and left. Everything looked very real. Satan was nearly an ordinary man; that was which Seraphim had not expected. He was ready to fight the Devil with a fiery sword, he imagined him to be a tremendous adversary. But it turned out that he was an adequate, modest and consistent man. Seraphim would not have believed in the existence of the Devil if it were not for teleporting from Abkhazia to Switzerland in one second, straight to *Zur Meise*. He also recalled how Cain got shot in the stomach, and survived without any doctors' help. He understood that he communicated with a higher mind, a higher power. Seraphim took off his old mantle, and repeated Cain's favorite water procedure; he folded his palms, took handfuls of ice-cold water from the washbasin and splashed it onto his face. Seraphim noticed that Archibald's water was also very clean and tasty. He took a sip of water and looked at the aluminum label on the wall, where something was written in German. Probably about the origin of water. Everything was fine. Seraphim took off his clothes and climbed into a large bathroom, with a big whirlpool. He opened the tap and water poured from all the faucets, warm and pleasant water. The bathroom was not ordinary. Seraphim recovered very quickly in the *Jacuzzi,* he felt relaxed and pleasantly tired. He wiped his miserable exhausted body with a white fluffy towel and fell onto a soft clean crispy fresh bed. The Morpheus instantly took possession of Seraphim.

'God created everything, and me, and this bed, and Lucifer! God is with us always!' This was the last thought of Seraphim before he plunged into a deep sleep.

Meanwhile, Archibald was comfortably seated in an armchair, while Cain stood near the fireplace and looked into the fire.

"You care about a drink?" Archibald offered.

"I don't want to; those drinks cause me a heartburn, as if I were drinking hot tar. I want to drink from the river, as in good old times."

"You have not yet seen the House of the Lord! My son, if you would have just once seen it with your own eyes, you would not be able to live in this shit."

"THEY will never take me to THEMSELVES; there is the entry for angels and the Chosen Ones only."

"Right you are, we will never see THEM again, although I can humbly wangle an invitation, but as an unwanted guest. I feel unwell after that, so it's better to find joy here in this garbage lot."

"What if there are still worse worlds?"

"Of course, there are. The Lord God, Allah, THEY created many different worlds, among them there are words similar to Paradise, to the Lord's House, and there are dreadful and tormenting like hot tar. Every soul gets what it deserves; everything is honest, no cheating.

"Tell me, Archibald, tell me the truth, you know the truth, what will happen to me and my friends? My friends who had died, where are they now?"

"I swear to you by all you want, I do not know. They disappeared immediately. This happens when THEY take a soul, and I do not know where they are now, honestly."

"And what will happen to me? You know?"

"You will always be with me. I asked that, and THEY allowed that."

"But if THEY change THEIR mind and turn me into a common mortal? Or turn me into a pig for my sins?"

"THEY will not transform you; we do not do anything against THEIR WILL. We are hooligans; and if I am not allowed to do something, then you first will know about it. We do not do anything against THEIR WILL, so we do nothing to turn us into pigs. We serve God, people do not understand that."

"I reflect on a question, why do we need this Seraphim? He presents a considerable problem."

"Come, come; everything will be fine. Tomorrow, you will define the difference between believers and non-believers, and then we'll decide."

"The DNA difference should be defined and the virus must be created."

"No need to hurry. We must do everything calmly and deliberately, so that we can stop at any time. Is Seraphim afraid of death?"

"You know, faithful to God are waiting for death as for a holiday, they are waiting for death with joy. Seraphim is the same."

"Splendid."

"Tomorrow we have to meet this brat Robert Bauman in *Bayer's* office, this is far away."

"Okay, the plane flies there. You'll get there in an hour. Or you want to use my demons' flight service?"

"No, it's only for emergency cases. I'll fly by plane."

"You have your own private plane, you have everything. Why do you still keep asking me? Why do you have to buy tickets, wait at the airport? You often surprise me! You, Cain, Son of Adam! You are not only the richest, but also the most influential person on the Earth, and you ride in public transport! You don't have to ask anyone about anything! You are your own master. We have one goal with you, to change this world! Call your crew, and your personal Boeing is immediately waiting for you, and the Rolls Royce is already waiting at the door. You need my demons, say, and I will give them to you in service, as I gave them to King Shlomo."

"I love to walk among people. Money and power do not interest me; I do not need luxury. I want to go to God, so that THEY give me peace. Mundane fuss is not interesting to me."

"Deserve it."

"Then instruct me how to do this, tell me."

"If I knew, I would not be sitting here at this garbage lot."

"Say, Archibald, maybe let's just change a little the Earth's trajectory?"

"This is not allowed."

"The project will take a lot of time and the result is uncertain. Where is the guarantee that this laboratory is able to create such a virus?"

"Do not worry, they have created many viruses, the problem was that those viruses were blind and killed everyone indiscriminately. The Germans have invented a virus to kill only people of a certain race, but, God loves to joke, THEY had mixed up all races long ago, so the virus mutated, and began to kill everyone."

"This is a complicated task."

"There is nothing complicated here. With your abilities, connect the world's best scientists and get down to work."

"Fine. I'm going to ponder over it in calmness."

Archibald knew that Cain was not sleeping, but did not argue; he answered, "Good night, my son."

Cain had his own apartment with all amenities on the second floor. There was his favorite capsule. He eagerly entered his apartment, and went into the bathroom; his capsule opened automatically and he lay down. The capsule was controlled by his voice only.

"Welcome, Dear Cain, what program do you choose?"

"All up to the fifth gradually."

"At your service."

The recovery container's transparent lid shut softly, and Cain closed his eyes.

Seraphim woke up; it was very difficult to get out of bed, for a long time he had not slept so tightly and sweetly. It was time for the night prayer; Seraphim washed himself with icy water, he was already accustomed to getting up at night for the prayer and was moving automatically. He knelt down, concentrated and turned to the earnest solemn prayer.

"God, the Creator, be with me. I beg You, Lord, destroy my body and my soul if I stumble. Forgive me my communicating with Lucifer. Creator of Worlds, forgive me."

Seraphim's forehead touched the floor; he opened to God his heart and soul.

There was a knock at the door. Seraphim kept on kneeling and praying. Someone was patiently standing behind the door. Seraphim finished his prayer, raised, went to the door and opened it.

"Seraphim, do I distract you?"

"Cain, son of Adam, I have a night prayer time."

"May I come in?"

"Come on in."

"The night prayer, it is very good; but how did you get up from this bed? In this bed, even I sleep."

"Is that kind of a special bed?"

"It is made for sleeping."

"I just got used to pray at night."

"The night prayer possesses an extraordinary power; the night prayer is like sacrifice. THEY immediately send the person a cleansing."

"Why do you keep saying THEY? Is it difficult for you to say God, Lord or the Creator?"

"Fine. I ask you what the gender of the word God is?"

"Male."

"Right. But are you sure that God is just masculine? What makes you think that God is a being like a human being? What makes you think that God belongs to a certain gender? Or do you think that God is some mighty tough guy, who had created the galaxies?"

"I imagine God as shining out of the fire, just and almighty."

"God is Energy without form and without sexual characteristics. Therefore, I always say THEY. THEY decide the fate of each soul, and if you are lucky enough, your soul will be attached to this energy, and you will go to the House of God, the World, which is ideal, the world that does not know sorrow, where a soul will raise into its highest state. That is what we all strive for. Moreover, this state is forever and ever."

"Do God hear me when I pray?"

"Everyone in this world hears you; that is why I came to you. Each prayer sends energy and the soul is healed and modified. It also affects your body and your physical state. Here you are, say, from the moment you started praying, did you ever get sick? You even had an accident and got away with only a scratch! Do you think this is a coincidence?"

"I know that God shelters me."

"God does not just shelters you, God imperceptibly altered you and you are no longer a simpleton and a desperado Lyonia; you are already a Chosen Seraphim."

"Where did you take all this from?"

"Can you read people's minds?"

"No. I feel people differently. It seems to me that I know a person for a long time and I guess how he will act in the future... something like that. I feel every person. It's true."

"Can you change the weather?"

"I can ask God, and God will give rain or heat. It happened so now and then."

"That means you are the Chosen one, an ordinary man cannot do that."

"I don't do it, God does it with the weather..."

"Well, you understand me, you are different, and we will find the difference."

"Are you also Chosen?"

"Yes, I am Chosen, but not in the way I would like to be."

"Are you damned?"

"Maybe."

"Do you pray?"

"No. I used to pray, but now I do not pray. For me personally it is useless."

"THEY don't hear you?"

"THEY punished me."

"What do you think, is it possible to change something?"

"I think that God left me to the End of Times, so we will try to bring this time closer."

"By means of this virus? All the same, many will survive, especially those of whom you will not benefit."

"The world is as it is, it is about to change, and this is already interesting. We can live in purity, at least for some time."

"Do you think you will be forgiven after this?"

"I think that THEY will make me a mortal man and this will already be a step forward. I will sleep at nights and have dreams; I will feel the taste of morning coffee and fresh apple pie. Maybe I would be able even have children and grandchildren, and I will play football with them. I will forget all the nightmares that were in my former life. The Almighty can do this; at least His Angel has already threatened me with this prospect. Becoming a common man would be better for me than remaining immortal, without sleep and without a personal life. I am tired, and I want a change, even for the worse."

"Clear. You want to provoke the Almighty to act against you?"

"Right. You go to bed; today we fly to Germany."

"Good night."

Cain quietly left the room. Archibald heard every word and did not like this conversation. He did not want to part with Cain; he was used to him. Therefore, Archibald decided to alter the initial action plan. He whispered, "Urmas!"

Only the Most High God owns time; but on the Earth God granted Lucifer the right to act in his own discretion and rotate time.

Seraphim woke up in the embrace of a beauty, he could not recognize the place, and the spacious bed where he slept, he ran around the house, and it was a huge villa with glass panes overlooking the ocean. That was a real posh home.

Seraphim felt conned. He could not recall anything; everything was as if in a fog. He wandered around the house and saw a mirror, from the reflection a sporty muscular man, whom he had never seen before was looking at him. He came close to the mirror and could not understand anything, his appearance changed. A pretty girl came up to his side and asked him in English, "Darling, want some coffee?"

Seraphim, without any hesitation, kissed her on the cheek, and answered promptly and also in fluent English:

"Yes, baby, make it as usual."

He wanted to recall something very important, but could not. He went out into the courtyard and saw a huge pool surrounded by a beautiful landscape; he ran barefooted on the gravel and dived into the crystal clean blue water. "What a beauty," Seraphim thought. "And I even forgot my name. In principle, never mind, it does not matter!"

In the morning, Cain called the airport and demanded to prepare his private Boeing; he also ordered his car to the entrance. All those who served Cain enjoyed unusual privileges; they set on their own the salaries for themselves and, if necessary, could always demand the needed sum from the bank. Cain carefully and for a long time selected his team. They all were extremely honest and loyal people who were ready to serve him at any time. Cain did not spare anything for them for their faithfulness, in principle, he himself printed money, so it would be very stupid to spare paper for his devoted team. After he had planned his way to Leverkusen, Cain decided to wake Seraphim. He knocked lightly on the door; there was no answer. Cain opened the door and saw that there was no one in the room. Crumpled bed, on the floor near the bed he noticed a wooden cross. Cain went to the bathroom and saw locks of hair in the washbasin.

"What for did he shave?" Cain said aloud. "What's happened here?"

Cain began to run between the bathroom and Seraphim's bed; he was looking for a trail.

"Where are you? Bastard, why did I not kill you then right away?"

His eyes were dimmed with tears of anger, his expectations shattered into dust. Archibald gives hope, then takes it back and thus breaks a person's heart.

That was what has happened to Cain. It seemed to him that with Seraphim's help he would solve his problems.

Archibald sat in his comfortable chair and grinned.

'Jerk!' Archibald thought.

Cain burst into the fireplace room. "This wretch has disappeared! Ran away, asshole!"

"Maybe he was just scared? We'll call the police and tell them to find out, because I do not see him."

Cain could not calm down; he was cruising around the hall at a quick pace and held his head in both hands, "Sonovabitch!"

"Quit raving, we will find him now."

"But how?"

"Urmas, tell me where Seraphim is?"

"Master, he ran out into the street, and was knocked down by a car. Died on the spot. He lies there in the city morgue. They classified him as a monk's unidentified body."

"Well, there you are! And you were afraid! We have found him!" Archibald rubbed his hands with unabashed delight.

Cain stood like a marble statue, he clenched his fists, and tears were running down his face. Archibald stood with his back to Cain; he knew that Cain was crying and that he was very hurt. But as if nothing had happened, he went on, "Don't you worry, we'll invent something else. We'll take his DNA, anyway, there is his body in the morgue, and that is the actually the DNA we need."

Cain could not talk, he had a lump in his throat, he cursed himself, he hated himself. It was very painful. He regained composure and squeezed out, "How did it happen? Where was he going? Why did he run out on the road? Give me the answer Archibald, you are the Master here on the Earth and nothing happens without your permission!"

"You forget Cain, The Lord is God, I am just THEIR servant. You know that, I do not decide anything."

"Do not lie to me, Archibald, you know everything perfectly well, tell me the truth!"

"You're upset, I understand you. You would not believe me anyway. Urmas said he decided to go to the brothel before the end of the world. He got in touch by phone with a call girl and demanded some carnal pleasures. We find it hard to believe. But when we go to the morgue, we will find his corpse, and, I think, the reasons for his escape."

"Why are you shooting me this bull? He got up at night prayer, and then ran after a broad? Do you think I have chicken brains?"

"Not exactly chicken, but sometimes one cannot foresee the actions of other people."

"I am a goddamned idiot! I got it! You have heard our conversation, and decided to kill him! Now everything is clear to me!"

"For what reason should I kill him?"

"You didn't kill him; you neatly dispatched him, cast his soul somewhere far away, and tossed up to me the body, so that I would believe in that bullshit."

"You know, I cannot kill anyone without the permission of the Lord."

"I still don't know how, but I know well your hand! You're involved in this somehow."

"Tell me, what's the reason for me wanting him to die? You do the maths."

"I am going to find him anyway."

"THEY took him to THEMSELVES; I do not know where he is."

"Well, I'll find him anyway."

"It is only if God prompts you."

"Someday I will find out anyway."

"Let's go to the morgue and collect the corpse. Can you fly to Leverkusen with the body tomorrow?"

"I think that this cooperation should be suspended."

"You don't want to work anymore on this project?"

"I want to, but I will not fly with the corpse, spare me that delivery."

"Okay, we will send the body separately by mail."

"Well, while it's still morning, I'll go to the morgue to identify the deceased and process the necessary documents."

Archibald nodded and turned away, hiding a grin of triumph.

A month of a quiet relaxation on the ocean beach passed imperceptibly; Seraphim enjoyed the prodigal life of a rich playboy. He led a carefree lifestyle, but sometimes an incomprehensible sadness overwhelmed him. He visited an expensive shrink; he sought to recall his past. Seraphim tried to recollect his previous life under hypnosis. Nothing worked.

Then once, striding along the embankment, he saw some Hindu, a vagabond Yogi Fakir, who performed amazing tricks. Seraphim stopped and watched the Yogi, and when he finished his performance, Seraphim pulled out fifty dollars and handed the bill to the fakir. Fakir touched the money, and intently peered at Seraphim. Then he took his hand and said in English, "Are you in a strange body?"

Seraphim felt a frog in his throat and nearly fainted. 'Why did he say that? What did he mean?'

"Do we know each other? Have you seen me here before?"

"Did the evil spirits move you to another body?"

"I don't understand what you're talking about. I am John Harris; I have been living here for more than twenty years."

"Don't you remember where you're from?"

"I had memory lapses, but I am taking some medicine now."

"You do not need no medicines, you are healthy. Your old body is dead. You have a mission, and I will help you."

Seraphim pulled out his wallet, but the Hindu stopped him,

"This money is not that clean, I do not must to take it. This money is of RAHU! No good! And your body is RAHU business! If he hear us, then both of us is finish."

The Hindu pulled out some red powder from his bag of and sprinkled it on his head, then took another handful of red powder and sprinkled it on Seraphim's head too. Seraphim's was dumbly surprised by the Hindu's strange attitude.

"RAHU is already here until he sees you. You are very important to him."

"What is Rahu like?"

"Rahu is an evil force."

"Why does she pursue us?

"He's following you, and he's going to kill you and me right away."

Archibald decided to have some fun and adopted the form of a police officer. He saw the Seraphim and the fakir and watched them. But then, when he saw that the Hindu had sprayed Seraphim's head with protective powder, he did not like it. Archibald did not want Seraphim to withdraw from the conspiracy and come to his senses. Therefore, he quickly approached the Hindu, "Your papers!"

"RAHU! RAHU!"

"Do you understand English? Present your documents; I am a police officer. You seem suspicious to me."

The Hindu silently stared at Archibald and did not even blink.

"Rahu, I wanted to help him. Let me go."

"I'll call the car and we will establish your identity at the police station."

Seraphim could not resist and intervened, "Officer, sir, what exactly you suspect this man of? What is your point? I'll call my lawyer now and your career will stop. You are a racist!"

"I advise you not interfere, otherwise I will arrest you too. No lawyer will help you."

Archibald took the Hindu by the wrist and told him, "Please, submit your documents and show the content your bag."

The Hindu wanted to wrench out and run away, but Archibald held him tight, he threw the Hindu to the ground and handcuffed him, the bag fell, and red powder spilled out of the bag. Archibald pulled out the radio and said, "This is patrol five six zero eight, I demand the reinforcements at Pacific Host. Situation fourteen-two. Undocumented suspect probably spreads narcotic substances."

The radio immediately croaked the answer, "Roger, reinforcement sent."

"Got it. Over."

The Hindu lay and did not move; but Seraphim did not calm down.

"On what grounds do you arrest him?"

"Do you see this powder? This is most probably scopolamine, a very dangerous drug, and he robs tourists using this method. People inhale the powder and fall into euphoria, get under the influence and this villain then steals their money."

"I gave him money myself, but he would not take it."

"He sought to gain your confidence, sir."

Archibald turned the Hindu's bag upside down and several credit cards and a gun fell on the asphalt.

"Now, do you see that?"

Seraphim was perplexed, he could so easily fall victim to a fraudster. He was glad that the policeman intervened on time.

"Will you testify, sir? We need a witness."

Seraphim felt unwell and was nauseous, and he thought that this was the effect of the powder which the Hindu sprinkled on his head.

"No, officer, I don't want to participate in this."

Seraphim proceeded his way of walking along the embankment; suddenly he had a strange feeling. The magic red powder neutralized and chased away the witchcraft; Seraphim felt nausea and threw up vehemently and violently. Then he tried to reach his villa as quickly as he could, but his legs failed him. Abruptly his head went spinning, and he nearly collapsed on the pavement. He crouched and covered his face with his hands. For a moment, he saw a flashback from somewhere of an unknown to him mountainous country and of a hermit's cave... Then he heard voices speaking to him in an unknown to him tongues…

Meanwhile, Archibald let the vagabond Hindu walk without charging him, and followed Seraphim. He altered his appearance again and embodied himself into a girl who sat every day on the same bench painting the same picture of the ocean waves.

The girl caught up with Seraphim, "Excuse me, you feeling unwell?"

"Mmm. Ahha... Yes. I am…"

"I have a drinking water, here; now, drink some and refresh your face. Is it paint on your head or dust? What is it? Let me pour some water on your head, you will feel better at once."

"I appreciate your aid, sincerely."

"My pleasure. Once it happened that a stranger saved my uncle in the street as thus. So I'm saving you and the world now," the girl smiled, and took to washing the dangerous mysterious red powder off Seraphim's head, while mentally cursing heartily 'that goddamned asshole shitty moron Hindu Fakir.'

Seraphim almost immediately felt better, he returned to his previous state. Nausea was gone and his head was not whirling anymore.

"That's better. How are you feeling? Let me wipe your head with a *water*."

"Thanks a lot, I'll do it myself. Let me buy a coffee or what can I do for you?"

"I'd be glad, I have half an hour, we can drink coffee together. Then I hurry to my classes. What is your name?"

"My name is John, John Harris."

"I am Susan. Just Susan."

"I am grateful for your help; your water really saved me."

"I really wanted to help you; I saw you were feeling unwell."

"Where do you study?"

"At the Medical College. My parents moved to Los Angeles because of my studies."

"Splendid, are you going to be a doctor?"

"There are a lot of doctors; I want to be a nurse."

"A nurse earns less."

"First I will become a nurse, and then I'll see. I am not after a high salary. Money for money is not the main goal."

"I am already obliged to you, so if you need a sponsor, I am ready to help you pay for the education. I would just return the favor."

"My grandfather can pay anything for me. It's okay."

Seraphim felt elated, good mood returned to him. He forgot the Hindu and his incomprehensible reminiscences. The *Dukes Malibu* brightened his day. It was an oceanfront restaurant made of wood. They sat at a table for two; the atmosphere was very romantic.

"What will we order?"

"A fruit salads and a cocktail".

Susan looked at the menu and continued, "I'll have a *Lava Flow* and a piece of lemon cake."

"And I'll just have a coffee."

Seraphim, alias John Harris, jumped up and went to the bar counter so as not to wait for the attendant. He approached the bartender and made an order. Archibald, alias Susan, sardonically watched him go. Archibald knew that the most effective weapon is lust and falling in love, practically every man in such a state forgets his main tasks and problems; that always works. It worked with Seraphim too; he forgot all his remembrances at once and switched to the pretty girl-student Suzanne. Archibald would send one of his girl servants to him, who would wind him round her little finger, and then he would forget about his uneasiness. Archibald had plenty of different restless female souls in the assortment who knew how to boob men. He decided to temporarily use the body of a young girl and then instill in her body the soul of a woman who in her past lives behaved unseemly. God does not give bodies to such people and they as a rule, become restless, they are tied to a cemetery or to their dead body. Archibald could manage them and summon them. He knew every soul by name. While Seraphim was talking to the bartender, Archibald mentally called out a soul, which was happy to return to a live body again.

'Ornella, that's the man, his name is Jack Harris. It is necessary that he falls in love with you and thinks about you only and exclusively. You will be with him until I call you off. If there are any oddities, think of me. I opened you a room, fly in. Discuss each venture with me. He is very important to me; do not let me down.'

Ornella flew into the body of the girl and very quickly entered the role of a student and mistress.

Archibald returned home to Zurich. At that time, Cain with Robert Bauman had been studying the Seraphim's body for a whole month. The body was special, it did not indulge in rotting; there was no usual process of decay. DNA analysis has already been performed, but the difference with ordinary human DNA has not yet been established. Seraphim was mummifying, but in this case, which was strange, his features would not distort in shape after death. It was very surprising for scientists who studied the body of the late monk Seraphim. The process of decay has not even been started. The study of DNA will take much time. After all, the difference between human DNA and monkey DNA is one nucleotide, that is, one per cent only! And if you compare the DNA of the pig and the man, they are almost blood brothers. Transplantation of internal organs is already promising, and a pig theoretically can gestate pregnancy of a human embryo. If you look at a small, undeveloped pig embryo, you see that it has a face, and it has an initiation of a five-fingered hand and is nearly identically similar to a human embryo. Therefore, the difference between two human DNAs is not that easy to establish. But the outstanding German scientists worked 7/24 nonstop.

Once, during the *Third Reich* time, the German scientists also tried to bring out the ideal race, but the necessary precision technology was not yet developed, and they did not manage to solve this problem. But nowadays, the technique is a little higher advanced, although, as before, they could not succeed. Because only God permits a living cell to accept or not to accept another cell. In this case, Robert did not believe in God, he believed only in his own potential. Robert admitted what had already been proven, that it was possible to change human DNA by power of thought. A German scientist Guido Brandt conducted these studies, and he proved that the power of thought affects the DNA; respectively, Robert understood that prayer and a godly way of life should directly affect the desired change. Cain did not need scientific evidence, Cain knew that a person transforms instantly, he wanted to discover THE gene, which leads to mutation. Cain wanted to connect the Russian scientist Petr Garyaev to his studies, but he turned out to be a tough guy, and decidedly rejected to participate in their research. Thus, this Petr Garyaev also proved that the human DNA like a magnetic tape, carries and records all information. Also, it has been scientifically proven that training the brain and stimulating certain areas of it can drive value on health.

Scientists have tried to understand exactly how these practices affect the human body. New research brought the first evidence of specific molecular changes in the body, which occur after intensive meditation and prayer.

Robert was elated; he obtained the first evidence. The results of meditation and prayer in the group of experienced meditators and the effect with a group of untrained subjects who were involved in quiet, non-meditative activities induced everyone into delight. After eight hours of uninterrupted meditation and prayer, genetic and molecular changes were discovered in meditator's tissues, including changes in gene regulation and reduction in levels of anti-inflammatory genes that are responsible for physical recovery after stressful situations. Robert immediately reported this good news to Cain, and they all together decided to listen to the Professor Davidson's account.

Davidson also belonged to Cain's team, because he devoted his entire life to the study of the human DNA.

"As far as we come to know, this research for the first time demonstrates instant changes in gene expression among the subjects practicing meditation and prayer!"

Robert was delighted with the results.

"The most interesting aspect is that changes are observed in genes that are currently subject to anti-inflammatory drugs and analgesics."

Cain smiled triumphantly; he gathered the needed and proper team. They all boasted to each other until this conversation and laboratory results were published in the *Psycho-Neuro-Endocrinology* magazine.

At this point Cain flared up and summoned Robert.

"Immediately develop a 'non-disclosure' agreement and make everyone sign it! I do not need no goddam advertising!"

"You got it, *Chef,* that will be done instantly."

"Did you read what they wrote? They sent the results of our analysis to different institutions, here, read!"

Cain extended the center spread to Robert.

"It has been found that meditation and prayer have a positive effect on inflammatory diseases and is approved by the American Heart Association as a preventive intervention. New research results may demonstrate the biological mechanism of its therapeutic effect."

"Do you see that? They will now use our methods for treatment and then our work has gone down the shit pipe!"

"I apologize, *Mein Herr*, we did not warn them that it was prohibited to spread. They will sign a contract and this will not happen again!"

"I really hope so. I do not need common people heal themselves with a prayer or meditation! Your whole *Bayer* will collapse, and I will lose my influence on the masses! People **MUST** buy our medicines, but **NOT BE TREATED FREE!** That can break the system! **DO YOU UNDERSTAND, MORON?**"

"Jawohl, Mein Herr! I did not think about the consequences!"

"You, idiot, if people seriously believe, then WE ARE FINISHED, we will become nothing! Do you understand this? It is necessary to make an instant **REFUTATION** so that people take it as a nonsense!"

"Jawohl, Mein Herr! I will get in touch with the right journalists right away!"

"GET LOST!"

Cain opened his laptop to read the news and immediately picked up a fresh article, *"Gene activity may vary depending on perception"*.

Cain opened the beverages cabinet, took a cigarillo, lit it nervously and continued to read, *"Simply put, this means that in order to treat cancer, we must first change the way we think."*

Cain smoked, puffed out a lot of smoke and pondered. He was really afraid that people would start learning prayers prematurely and heal themselves with prayers. He was afraid of losing his influence on people, he was not afraid of losing money and closing the main medicines production factories, he was afraid that people would be ahead of him and able to escape.

He read further.

"Our mind's function is to reconcile our beliefs and real experiences. This means that your brain will regulate the biology of your body and your behavior according to your beliefs. If you are told that you will die within six months and your brain believes it, then most likely you will die during that time. This is called the "nocebo effect", the result of negative thoughts, the opposite of the placebo effect."

Cain was upset, but his only consolation was that common people would never read this highly sophisticated article, and moreover, believe it.

Cain hoped for good luck.

Although hope is the main Archibald's instrument.

Cain was determined to buy that vehement Dr. Bruce Lipton so that his delirious ideas would no longer spread.

He proceeded reading.

"Dr. B. Lipton says, 'It has long been known that two people may have the same genetic predisposition for cancer. But one disease manifested itself, and the other — no. Why? Yes, because they lived differently: one more often experienced stress than the second; they had different self-esteem and self-perception, different train of thought. Today I can say that we are able to control our biological nature; we can, with the help of thought, belief and aspirations, influence our genes, including the processes occurring at the molecular level. In essence, I did not invent anything new. For centuries, doctors have known the placebo effect — when a neutral substance is offered to a patient, claiming that it is a medicine. As a result, the substance actually has a healing effect. But, oddly enough, a scientific explanation of this phenomenon has not yet existed."

"Dr. Lipton stated that it all comes down to the fact that the subconscious, which contains our deepest convictions, was programmed. Ultimately, it is these beliefs that become priorities." 'This is a difficult situation,' says Dr. Lipton. 'People are programmed to believe that they are victims and that they have no control over the situation. They are programmed from the very beginning with the beliefs of their

parents. So, for example, when we get sick, parents tell us that we need to go to the doctor, because the doctor is an authority that cares about our health. As a child, we receive from parents a message that doctors are responsible for our health, and that we are victims of external forces that we are unable to control ourselves. It's odd that people are getting better already on their way to a doctor. That's when the innate ability to heal oneself dies, another example of the placebo effect."

Cain picked up another periodical from a coffee table and nervously thumbed through it. The name of Dr. Lipton stroke his eye again. Cain crumpled the magazine and threw it on the floor.

'We **must** entice this famous Dr. Lipton to our project, he is very smart, we must understand with whom he communicates in our laboratory and then invite him and shut him up.'

Cain pressed the button and called Robert, after some seconds later, Robert knocked on the door.

„Mein lieber Herr, darf ich herein?"

"Robert, have you prepared a 'nondisclosure agreement'"?

„Jawohl, Mein lieber Herr, our lawyers have already prepared everything."

"I need the truth, so don't you even try to lie to me! Remember, I see you through! Do you know such a so called, *Dr. Lipton?"*

"Mein lieber Herr! Personally, I am not acquainted with him, but I heard of him a lot. I think we are a good team."

"You're not here to **think,** I gave you the money to **buy** all the best scientists, and you **screwed** it! Who knows PERSONALLY that GLORIOUS DOCTOR LIPTON?"

"Mein lieber Herr! Our Professor Davidson communicates with Dr. Lipton, and keeps friends with him."

"Is he the one who transmits the results of our research to Dr. Lipton?"

"No, sir. I do not think that our professor is engaged in espionage, he could just share information for other reasons. He is an altruist, and would never sell something, that can save millions of people."

"He works with us, thus the results of our work are a secret for everyone. Warn everyone not to tell anyone anything from now on. We were the first, we proved that Seraphim changed the structure of its DNA, and its cells, so much so that his body does not rot and does not even smell. We were the first, and I do not want other scientists to discuss the results of our work."

"Of course, sir! Should I meet with Dr. Lipton?"

"Yes. Offer him whatever you want, but he must work with us and the contract must also be signed."

"May I go?"

"Dismissed."

Cain pulled out another cigarillo and lit it.

An uneasy feeling of anxiety overwhelmed him, something was wrong. He felt that he had missed something.

"*Tovarishch* Lenin!"

A thick stench of rotten rags filled the office.

"Yes, Master, I'm listening to you."

"Ask Archibald, if I can talk to him."

"Archibald is ready to talk with you at any time, Master."

"Volodya, just go and ask."

After a few seconds, Cain heard a voice in his head, "Yes, my son, what do you want?"

"Archibald, tell me what is going wrong?"

"There is one person in your team who collects information and sends the results of your work to all scientific institutions."

"Who is he?"

"This is your precious Robert. He wants universal recognition, as the first scientist who will change the world. He wants to become famous and get the Nobel Prize in medicine."

"Damn! I will kill him and that's it."

"You still need him."

"But what am I supposed to do?"

"Let's put him in a frame. I will punish him slightly, and he will sit tight. Since he does not believe in God, then his fate is in my hands."

"Splendid, I regained a healthy sense of self-confidence."

"Be in touch at any time, I will prompt and support. Take care!"

After the conversation, Cain collected his personal belongings and went home. The only thing Cain thought about all the time was that he only thought of God. Cain lived in a house near the laboratory; he rented a spacious house with all the amenities for himself to be distracted sometimes. Cain sat on a large couch, turned on the TV, and closed his eyes.

Robert Baumann got into his luxurious Mercedes and moved along the road with a pleased expression of self-congratulation on his face. He dialed the number of his beloved wife, but the phone was off line. Robert thought that maybe her phone was dead. But thoughts piled up, mostly uneasy questions, a strange voice whispered directly to his brain, 'She cheating on you with someone else. Locate her car and find out who she is sleeping with.' Robert's face has changed and his face has become very serious. These treacherous thoughts did not leave him, and he pondered where his wife was. Robert decided to go home. His house was empty. He turned on the TV and switched channels, he did not like alcohol, but now he decided to drink. He poured himself a full glass of wine and drank. Ache in his chest did not pass; he searched with his eyes for a stronger drink and found brandy. He knocked over half a glass of cognac, and he felt hot, his brain began to throb, he pulled the phone out of his pocket and fell into a chair. His wife's cell phone was still turned off. Robert watched TV, but saw nothing and did not understand the words; he was expecting his wife. Suddenly, he heard a noise from a car pulling up; Robert jumped up and dashed to the window. His wife got out of the car, the car drove away. The entrance door opened and his beloved wife entered the house. Robert collected himself and tried not to betray his excitement.

"How was your day? I called you."

"I lost my phone. Without it, I cannot recall a single number. Here, I bought myself a new phone."

"And who brought you home?"

"This is Maria from my work; she and her husband gave me a lift. I'm going to take a shower; what will we have for dinner?"

"We can go to a restaurant."

"I'll be back and we'll discuss it."

His wife went to the shower, and Robert began to search his wife's pockets and her purse. He found a business card, there was written in beautiful golden letters, *Elite Swinger Club.* Robert's throat turned dry, at the bottom of the handbag he found her phone, it was just switched off. Robert turned on her mobile phone and at the same time turned off the sound, he began to read new messages about missed calls, and newly received messages. He opened some at random and saw photos of strange naked men. Then he saw in the gallery a recorded video. On the record were was a lot of naked men, and his beloved beautiful wife was lying on the table. Robert felt sick, the light darkened in his eyes, his temples drummed. He put the phone down and went to the bathroom, where his spouse was. The shower was on, he opened the door and felt his hands, his back and neck go numb, he had a feeling that he would drop dead right there. He slid aside the door of the shower, his wife saw him and said, "Come in, join me!"

He undressed and went to her shower; he hugged her and kissed her face. He did not know what to say to her or how to ask her. He was feeling really at a loss.

"Tell me, darling, how many men did you have before me?"

"You are my first man!"

"Yes, but you were not a virgin then."

"It happened to me accidentally, we gathered with girlfriends, and so I lost my virginity! This does not count!"

She laughed loudly and pressed herself against him. He felt not funny.

"Have you ever cheated on me?"

"What do you mean by cheating?"

"Sex with other men."

"Treason would be if I left you, and cool sex with other men is not treason."

He grabbed her by the throat, his fingers clenched tightly around her tender neck, she slapped him in the face, but he could not stop. Her lips turned blue, her eyes rolled up, her body went limp; his pretty wife passed away. He went out wet from the shower, came to the fireplace, poured himself a glass of brandy and drank. He felt better, as if the stone had fallen from his soul, the heaviness in his chest had passed. He thought what to do next. There were no ideas. Thoughts were gone. The first thing that occurred to him was to call Cain.

"Good night, Cai."

"Go ahead, Robert, I'm listening."

"I need your help; I don't know what to do."

"What's happened?"

"Can you come to me and see everything yourself?"

"Fine."

Cain knew very well what had happened at Robert's house. Robert behaved meanly, and Cain decided to teach Robert a lesson and put him in his place. He dialed the number of his friend police officer who served in another city, in Wiesbaden. His friend was a criminal police commissioner.

"Rudolph, hello, this is Cain, remember me?"

"Dear Cain, how are you doing?"

"Such a thing happened; a certain Robert Baumann strangled his wife in his house. He lives in Wiesbaden, works in the company *Bayer*; this Baumann's the only grandson of the old Baumann. Send people quickly; let them pack him."

"You got it; right away."

"Thanks and Good luck, see you."

"See you."

Cain stretched his fingers and smiled.

'Robert, Robert; who would have thought? And I remember how squeamish you were about people who were in prison, I remember how you said that only losers were in prison. Here it is, my dear Robert. Now it's your time to be in jail.'

Cain turned off the phone and sat down comfortably in his chair.

Robert waited for Cain, but he was not there, he began to ring, but Cain's phone was disconnected. Someone knocked on the door, Robert hurried to open, thinking that it was Cain. When he opened the door, four police officers stood on the threshold.

"Robert Baumann, we were informed that you performed a murder."

"It's some kind of mistake."

"Excuse me, where is your wife?"

"She is not home, she left."

"Stay here while the officers will check your house."

Robert broke away and rushed to the entrance; he was quickly caught up and arrested. His wife was found dead in the shower and the police sent her body to the morgue. In this case, everything was clear. Robert could not calm down; he hired the best lawyer. The lawyer advised to confess and tell the truth. Robert Baumann ended up in a detention facility. He could not be released under house arrest. Cain contributed, and the most active journalists found out about this incident. The next day, all the newspapers wrote about the murder, showed it on TV and discussed on the radio. The reporters ripped Robert Baumann to pieces. Cain wanted this arrogant and self-confident young man to fall to the very bottom in order to change for the better.

<u>For pain and grief improve any person.</u>

Only a beaten person understands another one beaten up, only a hungry man understands a hungry man. <u>A well-fed person does not understand anyone.</u>

"Let him serve time," thought Cain, "it will benefit him." Time passed, day after day, month after month, and there were no new results, the research stopped. Cain often sat in his house on the couch and pondered. Then one evening Archibald materialized in front of Cain. Cain was really scared.

"What happened?"

"I decided to share some important information with you personally. This is what I am telling you so that we can eliminate possible information leaks. Have you heard of such a *Maharishi Effect*?

"No. What is it?"

"This is when a group of people have gathered, and they meditated on peace. And when all people began to meditate on peace, military conflicts and crimes diminished significantly in this region. I am telling you this that they know the right way, and if they get more confirmation from your research, then we have nothing more to do here. People themselves will reach the necessary knowledge through meditation, and if they even begin to pray, then in principle for us this is the result and the end of our work. Very quickly everything will change and people will begin to change themselves, even without our participation."

"So, maybe it is better to publish the results and then this too will be a complete change of the world? We need purification, don't we? They will cleanse, change their DNA and live like bees. This is also suitable for us."

"Suitable, but it takes a lot of time. In principle, you can distribute all your secrets, so people can grow wiser faster."

"Look, some famous American scientist has proved long ago that we can mentally influence our DNA, and no one took it seriously.

"Do you mean Dr. Bruce Lipton?"

"Yes. Many people know him, but they do not believe in his statements."

"People are very stupid creatures; they are afraid of taking responsibility, they are waiting for miracles. God sends them the Scriptures, sends people, but they would no longer believe."

"I thought about going to America and bringing this Dr. Lipton to us."

"This is a good idea. Get Robert Baumann out of jail, he was trying to hang himself for the second time. I don't need him, but you'll need him, I've already broken the rope twice. Go and save him. He seems to have calmed down, does not want glory, he just wants back to mom."

"I will call the necessary people."

Cain pulled out the phone and called his banker in Frankfurt am Main.

"Abraham, my brother. Shalom! This is Cain; do you remember me?"

"Shalom, dear, how can I forget you, what can I do for you?"

"Call the Minister of Justice and everyone who's needed to release Robert Baumann immediately."

"Okay. I'll do everything necessary."

Cain put the phone down, and Archibald smiled and said:

"Is that all?"

"Yes. Regard Robert already free."

"So selected Jews rule the world and resolve all problems?"

"It is so; they stand right after God and after you. Jews keep the laws and God gave them the right to rule others."

"Yes. You are right, I have no authority over them, most of them realize God and they pray and follow all the rules."

"Although Islam is a perfect religion too. The Qur'an is the most understandable holy letter. The Qur'an is the best book that I held in my hands."

"I prevented Islam from developing, because Islam people immediately felt intimacy with God, and they began to change, I did not like it, and I invented various intrigues. So I will soon destroy all Islamic states, Muslims bother me, because the person who adopted Islam changes instantly, and I don't like it. For whom did I build eateries, restaurants, distilleries, tobacco factories, pharmaceutical plants? All this will be destroyed by the Muslims; they will follow the Commandments, and therefore I will destroy the Muslims. Muslims are terrorists; I will fight terrorism!"

"Then Christian people will be afraid of Muslims and will fight with them?"

"Yes, I will make everyone hate Muslims."

"That is if God will allow you."

"So far THEY are silent; I have many fallen souls who will be foaming at the mouth on television about sick Islam and sick Muslims. They will turn it around the clock until the whole world believes it.

"Yes, if everyone becomes Muslim, then there will be no poverty, there will be no orphans, there will be no alcoholics and drug addicts, they won't smoke like they smoke today, they won't eat at *Mac Donald's*, and they won't drink *Coke*. They will be much healthier, so they will not need medicines either. Yes, Islam must be destroyed! This is also going to afflict the drug business and prostitution. Yes, this is not at all fair. And what will you do now?"

"First thing it is necessary to bomb the Muslim capitals; we must kill all Muslims who live well. Come up with a blatant lie and under the fictional excuse kill everyone. I don't need them here on the Earth. I want to level Syria with the ground! Let's see what happens. You see, they pray five times a day! God makes them strong, God changes their DNA, one Muslim believer is equal in strength to fifty American Special Forces guys. God gives them knowledge and power. And when I kill them, God does not return them to me, they go straight to God. That's what pisses me off, they fear nothing but God, and happily go to their death, knowing that God will take them away. And I cannot help it. Additionally to all my problems, we need to fight Islam.

"But maybe let's go the other way around? Say, we develop Islam and then God will forgive us?"

"We will not be forgiven, you will simply do well to others, and we will not be better off from this. If everyone here were a Muslim, then whom will we rule? We need simpletons; we do not need Muslims! We need slaves and fools!"

"Coming back to our topic. If we manage to create a virus, then it also cannot kill Muslims."

"No, this virus will not affect Muslims, they pray and believe; they have been different for a long time, your virus will not kill them."

"Will it kill everyone who works for us and serves us?"

"Yes, everyone who serves me."

"Then why do we need this?"

"We serve God, although people do not understand this."

"THEY want those victims?"

"Yes, God is tired of the smell of roast pork; THEY want to quietly and without unnecessary noise remove unnecessary people."

"But what to do with the Seraphim's body? Bury it?"

"Obviously. Bury and forget."

Cain again fell into the sofa, he thought, what a hard day it was. He decided to watch TV and turned on the news. The news showed Russia and the conflict with European countries. Cain knew the truth. After the collapse of the Soviet Union, the military and the bandits took control of the former country. There was a special unit *Vympel*, and other military organizations, the Chechen group also took its place in the Kremlin. The time of rotten alcoholics was gone, and power has passed to sober greedy people. Naturally, Russian politicians were placed in plain sight so that the masses would not revolt.

Meanwhile Robert sat in a prison cell. He heard footsteps down the hall and heard the keys clinging. The door of his camera opened, the warden stood on the threshold.

"Robert, you have powerful friends, they asked you to immediately get you out of prison. There are several options. The first is the fastest; you die in the cell, we verify death, replace your body with another, and walk right now. We make you other documents, and you are free. The second option, we recognize you as mentally ill and transfer you to a sanatorium, where we will support you for a year, and then let you go, then you can retain your name and last name. The third option, you withdraw your plea of guilty, and we will look for those who killed your wife. This option takes a rather long time."

"I choose the first option; I want to leave this place at once."

"Well, let's go then, you have to cut off any connection with all your friends and relatives. We will place you in Cain's house; he will prepare everything for you. We will make you a small operation on the face, and then real papers."

"I agree to everything, just get me out of here, away from these damned walls."

"Good, Cain is waiting for you."

They walked along the corridor together, the prison was empty; Robert was looking for people in uniform, but there was no one. Robert was escorted to the service yard, where the car was already waiting for them. The car door opened, and Robert got into a car with police license plates. The big six-meter gate opened wide and the car drove out. Robert did not take his eyes off the window; he could not believe that he had escaped. Cain saved him. Of course, he could forget about the career of a scientist. He lost everything, family, money and his social status. If Cain pulled him out, then he had at least a job left. The car drove straight to Cain's house. There was a man standing at the entrance and he waved his hand, giving a sign that he was ready to open the door. The door of the police car would not open from the inside, so the stranger turned the handle, and Robert went out. He stood and breathed fresh air, a smile appeared on his face.

'Freedom! This is the most valuable thing in our life,' Robert thought. He went into the house and entered the hall, where Cain was already waiting for him.

"Well, hello Robert! Now you are free!"

"I appreciate it, *Mein lieber Herr*!"

"Yes, then I did not have opportunity to help you, only now it has appeared."

"Thank you, sir, I owe you."

"It's good that we made everyone sign the nondisclosure agreement, now you can work in the laboratory, and no one will know. I hushed everyone!"

"Did they sign the agreement?"

"Yes. Do you mind if we slightly correct your face? Your face needs a little change."

"I already heard that. If it is necessary, then it is necessary."

"I prepared a room for you on the second floor, you will live there."

"Is it possible that I have a computer or not?"

"Of course, there is a computer there. You're a reasonable man, and you will not expose me."

"I need a computer for work only, I am not going to write to anyone, and I will not enter my pages. I'm not a complete idiot. I do not want back to prison, this is a damn place!"

"Previously, you thought differently."

"I was a fool."

"That's a boy! You already understand, a little more, and you will believe in God."

"I already believe. We have proven DNA change from prayer! I learned the prayer *'Our Father'* and before your man came, I was kneeling and reading a prayer. Then I heard footsteps and they let me loose. This is not a coincidence; it was God who helped me out! God really exists and hears each of us!"

"Get out of here! Seriously?"

"I felt inside that God hears my prayer. God forgave me because I was stupid. Thank you Cain!"

"Okay, calm down. You are safe."

"If it were not for your research, I would never have come to God."

"Well done. But it's not God who saved you from prison, but me."

"God have told you that I need help. Otherwise, why would you need me? You have a good team, and experts and scientists in this field are by far better than me."

"Okay. Let's switch the topic. I'll prepare new documents for you, you will be a Swiss scientist. Tomorrow we will change your face."

"So, after the operation, I will have to rest until everything heals?"

"Tomorrow you'll be different!"

"URMAS! Take him to Archibald's *Zur Meise*, change his appearance according to the passport, which Archibald will give you, and put him in my capsule, let him recover."

Robert wanted to say something, but did not have time. His body and soul flew away to Satan. Archibald was surprised that Robert had flown to him. He thought what appearance to give him and decided that it was easier to transplant the soul, and to instill another soul into his old body. To do everything cleanly and without prevarication, he did not like bureaucracy. Archibald wanted to find an atheist scholar for whom no one would be sorry. He shared his thoughts with Cain, and Cain already knew that there would be no operation. He dialed the number of the warden who brought Robert and said, "You don't have to do anything, declare a jailbreak and put him on the wanted list."

"Are you sure? He will not be able to leave the country!"

"He has already left the country; do not waste time and resources."

Cain put the phone down and thought, "Why does Archibald need this Robert? Probably, he deserved personal attention! "

Meanwhile, Archibald picked up a young Swiss scientist who loved Darwin's theory, and who could spend hours talking about the Big Bang and the formation of the Universe. He was a very self-assured atheist who loved to tell raunchy jokes about Jesus Christ, about God and about the Devil. Archibald decided to joke too.

"Urmas, Radokan!"

His demon servants appeared; those were powerful demons, which could even change the Earth's orbit.

"Bring me Joachim Weise, who lives in Basel, a scientist, born on November 1, 1970."

Robert was shocked. He did not see such tricks even in movies. How could he move from Leverkusen in a second to Archibald's house? It was beyond all the laws of physics. A naked man suddenly appeared in front of Archibald.

"Hello Joachim, how are you? You are all wet! You were in the shower?"

"Yes. And who are you?

"I am the one about whom you constantly tell dirty jokes."

"Are you Jesus?"

"Hell! Do I really look like Jesus?"

Archibald lost interest in Joachim and turned to Robert, "Do you like him?"

"In what sense?"

"Do you like this body? You will look like him."

"I agree."

Archibald clenched his fists and closed his eyes. In an instant, Robert's soul flew into Joachim's body, and Joachim's soul vice versa flew into Robert's body.

"Just like that. Robert, meet Joachim Weise."

Robert stood naked and wet; he could not understand what had happened to him. He exchanged bodies with another man. Archibald did not pay attention to his surprise and called the demon, "Urmas! Take this former Joachim and transfer him to Berlin to the railway station, where they will quickly find him."

Robert's body, in which was the soul of Joachim Weise, flew to the Berlin railway station. Robert stood naked in a strange body.

"Look Robert, consider that I have done the most successful plastic surgery for you, no one will be ever looking for you. Your body is now in Berlin, it will be arrested and put back to the jail, and then your body will be transported to a sanatorium. And your life is just beginning, and the girl you have, she is now preparing dinner. I'll bring you back to the bathroom. You will remember everything yourself, tomorrow we will invite you to work in our laboratory, and you will return to work with us."

"Now I understand you! Forgive me for having been living wrongly, forgive me silly jokes about God, and joked about you, forgive me! I was stupid! I thought that I was the *Master of Life*!"

Robert collapsed to his knees, tears streaming down his cheeks. He muttered, "**God IS**, and Satan is standing here. O Lord, forgive me, fool."

"Robert, pull yourself intact. Remember, you are now Joachim Weise. You are Swiss."

Robert got up from his knees; he had a terrible look.

"Radokan! Take him to the apartment of Joachim Weise, from where you took this body, and put it there."

Robert has disappeared.

At this time, Cain was sitting at home on a cozy sofa and smiling. 'Obviously, they felt confident, they told nasty jokes, and now they both will be sent to the sanatorium.'

Cain did not want to see Robert; he irritated him. His German impassable stupidity haunted Cain; he almost hated him. Cain hated self-congratulatory people, and if

Archibald hadn't asked to pull him out, he would never have pulled him out. Cain knew that he began to pray to God in prison, but this was not enough for him. Cain could not forgive him. And now, if he works with him, he will crawl on his stomach, like the Nazis back in the forty-fifth. Germans, Austrians, Swiss, are such dogmatical nations, that as long as you don't give them a kick-off, they don't understand. Robert was a pure German.

Meanwhile, Joachim Weise ended up at the station without money and without documents. He understood that it would be difficult to explain everything to the police, but he would try and persuade them to believe him.

Patrol officers constantly combed the station in search of illegal immigrants. Joachim approached the patrol, "I am a Swiss citizen, I was in my bathroom at home, took a shower, then somebody brought me by force to Zurich, and from Zurich they threw me here. Help me get back home."

"Of course, we will help you. Let's go to the precinct, we need to establish your identity..."

Joachim Weise in Robert's body went to the police station.

Then they will fetch him to prison. In prison, he will look at himself in the mirror, and will shout that he is Joachim Weise, that he is not Robert Baumann. He will remember the brazen face of the young guy who did this to him. His words will be ever spinning in his head, "Well, how do you like my joke?" A year later, they will establish him in a sanatorium, where he will remain until the end of his days.

Meanwhile the work in the laboratory temporarily stopped; without Robert it was more difficult, as they say, one bad general is better than two bad ones... Cain needed a deputy. Archibald informed him that Joachim Weise will arrive the other day and will help arrange his work in the laboratory. Cain became irritable.

At that time, Joachim Weise, alias Robert, returned to the shower in his apartment, his girlfriend was waiting for him in the room, he vaguely tried to remember "his former other life." There were flashes and failures; there were no clear memories. He knew that he needed to go to Leverkusen to the laboratory, but there was no invitation, and he did not know how to contact Cain.

Suddenly, someone rang the doorbell, and Sabina went to open the door, "Joachim, it's for you!"

Robert went out into the corridor to the front door, a postman stood at the door, holding a letter in his hands.

"Mr. Weise, here's a registered letter for you."

"Thank you."

Robert approached, signed the form, and the postman handed him a letter. Then the mail carrier politely said goodbye and left; Robert closed the door and opened the envelope. Inside was an invitation for an interview at *Bayer*, Leverkusen. Robert smiled; he wanted to escape from this apartment. His girlfriend Sabina kept on asking lots of questions for which he had no answer.

"Sabina, honey, I'm leaving urgently, I have got a new job."

"So where are you going?"

"To Germany."

"I go with you."

"For now, darling it is not yet possible to go together, I'll take you away later when I sign the contract."

"Okay, I'll wait."

Robert frantically rushed to gather his belongings, he ardently wanted to leave this haunted house and return to his old life.

At that time, Archibald appeared before Cain.

"Hello my son. How are you doing?"

"The work has stopped for a while, although the gene is found! We need to develop a virus that will identify this gene and if it is not present in the body, then the process of decay starts up and the person gradually dies. A man begins to rot from within."

"Okay, so be it. Those are the ones, who tell jokes about God, and the jokes about us; they will rot. It fits me."

"But if they begin to pray, they will be saved."

"Before that, only a few people would guess. Now Robert goes to us."

Archibald disappeared and Cain was alone again.

Robert got into Joachim's car and drove to Germany. He calculated the distance on the navigator, only in six hours he will already be in his laboratory. In his head, Robert scrolled through the results and found a solution on how to determine the gene and how to launch the virus, he needed a laboratory computer.

Archibald sat in his vast armchair in *Zur Meise* and reflected on humankind, 'Human souls are the most stupid creatures, they believe in themselves, although their life, perhaps, is just a simple dream. They cannot distinguish the dream from real life, but no one thinks about it. They believe in their existence, although their whole life is just an ordinary dream in the Matrix. They quarrel, fight, cheat each other, lie, kill, and this is all just a dream, which is recorded and analyzed. This is a program of cleansing the soul from filth. God consists of pure souls, this is a tremendous energy, that has created an ideal world; and you must not enter this world in dirty boots. They believe in reality, they are astonished that a thought can change DNA. This thought is the only real part of their dream. Mentally, they can control both matter and time, and generally everything. But they do not know how, and do not even want to learn, a prayer to God would be the first step, people could change everything with their minds, because their life is a dream. All that they do is not real; all their lives are pure illusion, until they are completely cleansed.'

As it often happens simultaneously among kindred souls, Cain was sitting in his couch thinking, 'What if you change the trajectory of the Earth's orbit, if everyone dies, what will God do? Will he allow it? Because there has never been THE END OF THE WORLD, but what if I order a demon to tear the Earth off its trajectory? Now, if the Earth changes its trajectory by even one angle degree, everyone will die, and so will I. This whole story with the virus is very long; I need to check other options."

"Urmas!" There was silence, and nobody around.

"Urmas! Urmas!" Archibald appeared before Cain.

"You pulled me away from my thoughts. What do you want, my son?"

"I need Urmas, I want to check something."

"You forgot that I am not a man, and I know absolutely everything about you."

"Let's try, and check something."

"Move the Earth? Ha-ha-ha-ha! Your scientists have calculated the speed of the Earth, if you move it, then we will all perish!"

"I want just that, it is my purpose!"

"How can you move something that does not exist?"

"You want to say that we live in a collective illusion?"

"I never said that. I think God will not allow such destruction, never before has there ever been such a thing."

"Obviously; but what if we order Urmas and his partner to move the Earth?"

"Urmas submits to me, and I obey God, so I already told you. We will never have permission for such an action. It is impossible. Make a virus, fight for every soul. To kill everyone is preposterous, then no one will have a chance. We need to weed out the unsuitable from the good, although every soul is fit, they just need time to understand the sense. How can you tell a child at three years old that he is stupid and does not understand the laws of physics? Same with a young soul, it is not stupid, it is just a child, it needs to grow! And you want a three-year-old child to solve problems in astrophysics! This cannot be, the soul is a grain, it just sprouted, and you already demand the fruits! Every soul needs to grow up, go through school many times, and then, two or three hundred years later, the soul matures and can return to God."

"I do not understand it somehow. So what, not to make the virus? We are waiting until everyone is ripe?"

"This virus will frighten people and they will probably speed up their training, they will be striving for God and for knowledge. You won't kill anyone with this virus, you just scare them. Those who die will be reborn immediately. It just scares the little fools so that they will accelerate. And so, they will all remain here, just the values will change, they will learn to transfer knowledge mentally, they will feel the power of thought and will study it, they will learn to change their environment and reality by the power of thought. We will have less work."

"How long is measured for me?"

"You will be with me to the end."

"So I will never die?"

"No one dies, we are all immortal, people and angels, we just change the shell, as the snake takes off its skin. Therefore, people change bodies, but their soul is eternal. Especially stupid people are those who comply to sell their soul. How can you sell something that does not belong to you? The soul lives forever, and changing it for some rubbish, for a moment of glory or a couple of years of a quiet life, this is immensely stupid. Every soul belongs to God; God creates and teaches them. How can a child sell his mother for a toy? This is the same. We must be patient and direct those souls in the right way. I complicate them and confuse them, and they stay with me until they are fully enlightened."

"Archibald, I am enlightened, let me go. Please!"

"I don't take away the soul, only God takes it. And if you are still standing in front of me, then God has not taken you away yet."

"Fine. I see."

"Well, fine. Tomorrow your Robert arrives, work and invent! Create!"

"I will."

Archibald has disappeared. Cain fell to his knees and began to read a prayer, "Lord God, forgive me for all my sins. Punish me; kill my body and my soul. You are my

Creator; forgive me. Forgive me for my brother. Forgive me for everything! Give me the price; instruct me what to do, advise me the proper way!"

Suddenly Archibald appeared again in front of Cain:

"You constantly distract me! Why did you begin to pray again? You do not need it, you are the Chosen One!"

"I am not chosen, and from now on I will pray every day ten times a day."

"What for?"

"I want to be saved."

"The virus will not kill you, you have seen God, and therefore nothing can kill you."

"God will kill me. I will request THEM every day, and THEY will have mercy on me and I will be taken to THEIR place, or destroyed so that to shut me up."

"Is it so bad to be with me? I gave you everything."

"This is not a life, but a bad dream. Did you say 'school for the soul'? I finished school a long time ago. THEY just forgot to pick me up! I'm just a fool, who continues to believe you all the time!"

"Did I lie to you?"

"You are the king of lies!"

"I lied to you? Or you lied to yourself?"

"Archibald, I don't want to talk to you. Let's talk tomorrow…"

"Fine."

Archibald disappeared, and Cain, knowing that Satan cannot intercept his thoughts to God, continued to pray in his mind. He prayed all night without getting up from his knees. In the morning, he washed and continued to pray on his knees. The phone rang, he received a call from the laboratory; Robert, alias Joachim Weise, had already arrived at the laboratory. He waited for Cain. Cain got ready, got on his bike, and in fifteen minutes was already in the laboratory. In the office, he was already waiting for the updated Robert.

"Well, hello, Mr. Weise, how are you feeling in a new body?"

"Fine, younger and more handsome, I really like it."

"So, how about our project, have you already met our employees? Or greeted them?"

"I got acquainted with the team. I am so embarrassed to deceive them; I know everything about them, and everything that they tell me, I already know by heart."

"Be patient, all this is better than a sol."

Robert's face immediately changed, he understood his position."

"Indeed, I will not advise anyone to land up in jail. This is the worst thing that happened to me."

"You haven't seen real prisons; they distribute a glass of water a day in Thailand. You can wash, and you can drink, this is your right to choose. There are no sleeping places either, prisoners sleep on the floor in turn and have to pay for it."

"Have you been there?"

"I, unlike you, am interested in other people and countries. There if you would were caught in Thailand with drugs, then you would serve the life term."

"I will never go to Thailand."

"See, you have already made a mistake, you pronounced the word "never", which means that you will go. Now tell me you will "never" go to jail in Thailand! Say it aloud!"

"O Lord! God forbid! God save me from that!"

"And this is the right answer, not German. You grow up Robert. What did you remember about God? Are you an atheist?"

"I told you that I prayed a lot in prison. Moreover, we did the research ourselves. Prayer changes the structure of everything, changes not only DNA, but also water, matter. After this, I immediately learned the prayers and turned to God."

"Is that so? Well done. Believed, that means. Are you ready to die for faith?"

"Well, you ask the wrong person, I lost everything and even my body, I have nothing to lose. Tell me how and when, and I am ready, if it will bring results."

"Suicide never yielded results, the soul is reborn in another body and misfortunes continue. The self-murderer's soul does harm only to itself and to no one else."

"Well, maybe let's get down to work? I figured out how to identify a gene that changes the structure of DNA and matter."

"Robert, I'm glad you worked! When did you find time?"

"In prison. I was sitting in a solitary cell in silence and no one interfered with me, I was concentrating on my thoughts and so I developed a modified water molecular scheme, according to the same principle as we can modify the air molecular scheme. If we apply such water, we will be able to infect all people who will use water from reservoirs, and if we do it with air, then everyone who breathes air or would be caught in the rain, will be infected. I know exactly how to make a virus; a person will rot from the inside. Ammonifying microorganisms (otherwise, putrefactive microorganisms, putrefactive microflora) are widespread in the soil, air, water, animals, and plant organisms. Therefore, any suitable substrate is rapidly rotting. The genome that is formed from prayer destroys these viruses. Bacillus subtilis, Bacillus mycoids is controlled by the body's immunity, bacterial protein rotting is also a necessary part of digestion and occurs in the large intestine of humans and animals. Proteus activators are Proteus, Escherichia, rotting products that are constantly formed in the intestine (skatole, indole, etc.), cause chronic intoxication and are one of the causes of premature aging. And we will weaken the immune system and make an accelerator, so a person will rot alive."

"Very interesting. Obviously, a believer has unlimited immunity, while atheists have weakened immunity. But how do you explain that as long as a person is alive, one does not rot, but as soon as the soul leaves the body, it instantly begins to rot and stink?"

"I can try to explain it in such a way. Immunity is a constantly running engine that is powered by electrical energy, this energy is present in the soul, this is the biofield and low currents. That immunity resists all the bacteria, but as soon as the tension disappears, the engine stops, and the bacteria begin to multiply. The body begins to rot. The stronger a person believes, the more current and more immunity he has and the less bacteria. He has a higher conductivity of the current, he glows and gives off the energy that he receives from the ether. There are people like our Seraphim, who ruled both his immunity and bacteria, so they do not rot at all. God created them this way; they are no longer ordinary people, but super-beings that overmaster animals and all nature to themselves, influence the weather and the whole world."

"I see that you have thoroughly prepared for our work."

"In isolation, the brain works better and produces brilliant ideas. In our business, it is very simple, we will strengthen some bacilli, and ordinary immunity will not be able to fight them, we will immediately accommodate these bacilli to resist antibiotics, and then we will launch them into the water and into the air. A person will not be able to get protection in a pharmacy or from a doctor; there is no such medicine. For them, only faith in God remains. As soon as I create the infection, I will immediately try it on myself. I do not want to live, if my faith I am weak, I will eagerly give my life to God.

"You will survive. I already see; you shouldn't spend our viruses in vain."

"And they self-generate like a fungus. I will create a pair, and then they will multiply, so that will be enough for everyone."

"How much time do you need?"

"At most, a month."

"Go ahead and work."

Cain was pleased with such a breakthrough, he saw a simple solution how very effective bacilli, which are present everywhere, could be modified and then a person with a common immunity cannot survive.

A month later, Cain hired couriers, sent them to different countries, to all large cities. He launched the virus into all freshwater reservoirs and released modified oxygen. God has allowed Cain's idea came true.

Epilogue

Numerous people died from the virus, only true believers survived. Old Believers Christ, believers of Judea, the orthodox Jews, devoted Muslims – all these people survived. What happened next? Production stopped. The world has become cleaner. Banks and bankers disappeared, distilleries disappeared, snack bars disappeared, soft drinks with dead water disappeared; people stopped pumping oil and gas, and switched to solar energy. There were no more beggars, orphans, prostitutes, gays and drug dealers – they all disappeared. Tobacco plants, pharmaceutical factories have been closed. The market became different; there was no more stock exchange. Cain cleaned the world of filth and for the first time in many years, he did not smell the roasted pork. Did human souls think that their iniquity would be forgiven them?

We have to answer for all our bad deeds. The Earth is cleansed, and everyone lives according to the laws of the Lord, as it should be.

Amen!

www.ingramcontent.com/pod-product-compliance
Lightning Source LLC
Chambersburg PA
CBHW031334060726
47590CB00007B/2459